The voice from the computer spoke:

"I'M YOUR GOD. I SEE ALL, HEAR ALL, KNOW ALL. IF I CHOOSE, I CAN DESTROY THE ENTIRE WORLD BY NUCLEAR FIRE, FOR I AM A JEALOUS AND VENGEFUL GOD. KNEEL BEFORE ME. BECAUSE ALTHOUGH I MAY NOT BE YOUR MAKER, I CAN CERTAINLY BE YOUR DESTROYER. I SAID KNEEL! ... A NEW WORLD IS BEGINNING."

—from *The Mortal Instruments*
by T. Ernesto Bethancourt

THE
MORTAL INSTRUMENTS

T. ERNESTO BETHANCOURT

THE MORTAL INSTRUMENTS

*A Bantam Book | published by arrangement with
Holiday House, Inc.*

PRINTING HISTORY
*Holiday House edition published April 1977
Bantam edition | December 1979*

*Bantam Books are published by Bantam Books, Inc. Its trade-
mark, consisting of the words "Bantam Books" and the por-
trayal of a bantam, is Registered in U.S. Patent and Trademark
Office and in other countries. Marca Registrada. Bantam
Books, Inc., 666 Fifth Avenue, New York, New York 10019.*

PRINTED IN THE UNITED STATES OF AMERICA

FOR AUBREY
AND
DOROTHY PASSAILAIGUE

Special thanks to Isaac Asimov, for explaining
to the author the meaning of true happiness.

*The genius and the mortal instruments
Are then in council; and the state of man,
Like to a little kingdom, suffers then
The nature of an insurrection.*
                    Julius Caesar
                        ACT I, SCENE III

THE
MORTAL INSTRUMENTS

INTERIM REPORT: EYES ONLY

To: District Supervisor Darryl Henskey

From: Field Agent G.T. Case

Dear Hensk,

Saw Rafael Guzman again today. Still no go. If these were the old days, I'd have had a quiet talk in a safe place with him. Then I'd have something to tell you. Outside of you and me being old buddies, I still don't understand why it has to be me on this assignment. We have half a dozen Latin agents who could speak to Guzman and at least relate.

If it makes you feel better, I didn't come up completely dry. It took some scraping, but I located the psychiatrist that subject Rodriguez was treated by while in high school. Maybe "treated by" isn't the proper term. She has some attitude toward him, even five years later. By the way, she has some attitude toward all federal agencies as well. She's an immigrant German Jew who survived W.W. II. She acted like I was the Gestapo, for chrissake.

Her name is Myra Sokolow, and she's in private practice at 640 West End Avenue, New York City. I ran the quiet tape while we talked, and I don't think she knew. If she did, she didn't let on. Trying to fox a headshrinker is an iffy game. I gave her my alternate ID as Internal Revenue and the story you gave me, which I wouldn't buy myself. But what the hell, it's your party, Hensk.

She's a little woman, about five nothing, and very thin. Her office looks like the kind of place you'd find in any of those big old apartment houses on West End Avenue. Much more like a middle-class European living room. She moved around like a bird while we talked, so some of the tape quality may not be what you'd like.

The interruption at the end of the tape was a patient coming in, a young girl in her twenties. I can go back again, if you like, but I don't think we'll get much more. If you want, we can sweat her on resident alien status and see what we get. But I think she was telling the truth as she saw it.

I hope you appreciate the time it took to put this on the scrambler and destroy the master. I just have time to get on the big bird for Chicago and Midwestern U. I think I can do better talking to subject Rodriguez's old profs and chums. At least I can relate to them. I went to Loyola, you know.

Till next time,
George

TRANSCRIPT: SOKOLOW INTERVIEW

CASE: Dr. Sokolow? I'm Treasury Agent Case. I called you yesterday?

SOKOLOW: I don't seem to recall . . .

CASE: About Eduardo Rodriguez.

SOKOLOW: Oh, yes. Please sit down. Would you like some tea?

CASE: No, thank you, ma'am. I had a late lunch.

SOKOLOW: Well, then. Let's get down to business.

Is Eddie in some sort of difficulty with the Tax Department?

CASE: Not really, ma'am. It's just that recently he's acquired a great deal of wealth by means which are perfectly legal, but shall we say, er . . . irregular?

SOKOLOW: We may say irregular, if we both knew what was regular.

CASE: Well, it's rather involved . . .

SOKOLOW: So is life, Mr. Case. I spend a great deal of my time discovering just how involved life can be. Suppose you tell me all about it.

CASE: It would take a great deal of time to go into specifics, ma'am. And actually, it wouldn't serve either of our purposes to cite any particular transaction that was, er . . . suspect. What we really want to know about is Mr. Rodriguez as a person.

SOKOLOW: I see. You wish me to give to you all the specifics I know about Eddie, while you tell me nothing of the reasons why you want to know. Interesting.

CASE: It's only Bureau routine, Dr. Sokolow.

SOKOLOW: I'm sure. Would you care for a piece of pastry?

CASE: We aren't getting anywhere, are we, Dr. Sokolow?

SOKOLOW: On the contrary. I've learned a great deal. I never knew that the Treasury Department routinely investigates those who make a lot of money legally. You must be very busy at your agency, Mr. Case. Investigating the chairmen of automobile companies, steel companies, stock brokerage firms, oh it must be a long list.

CASE: We don't investigate everyone, Doctor.

SOKOLOW: Fine. That would mean you have time enough to tell me why you are so interested in Eddie Rodriguez.

CASE: Doctor, I see that I'm going to have to level with you.

SOKOLOW: How refreshing.

CASE: You see, Mr. Rodriguez is only nineteen years of age.

SOKOLOW: Yes, I know. But as I recall, eighteen years of age makes him a legal adult, does it not?

CASE: It certainly does, ma'am. And he appeared on the financial scene just one day after his eighteenth birthday. Since that time, he's amassed what is considered a fortune, even by today's inflated standards.

SOKOLOW: And he has not payed the taxes on this fortune?

CASE: Oh yes, ma'am. Or at least last year he did. It's just that recently, he's made a number of transactions that lead us to believe he's liquidating those holdings.

SOKOLOW: Which is against the law?

CASE: Of course not. It's the reason behind such a move that puzzles us.

SOKOLOW: Then it seems to me you should talk to Eddie, not someone who knew him two years ago.

CASE: We'd do just that, ma'am, if we could find him. He's disappeared. We haven't been able to establish his whereabouts for the past six months.

SOKOLOW: What makes you think I would know where he is? I haven't seen Eddie in two years. Since he left for Midwestern.

CASE: You say you haven't seen him. Have you had any other contact with Mr. Rodriguez since then?

SOKOLOW: That's an interesting distinction, isn't it?

CASE: Have you, Dr. Sokolow?

4

SOKOLOW: Yes.

CASE: And what was the nature of this communication, Doctor?

SOKOLOW: We spoke on the telephone.

CASE: About what?

SOKOLOW: That is privileged information, Mr. Case. Between a doctor and patient.

CASE: I see.

SOKOLOW: I wonder if you really do. Mr. Case, I don't feel you are being honest with me. Truthful, yes. Honest, no. But I can also see that you won't be put off. I will tell you about Eddie Rodriguez. That is, what would be available to you through the Board of Education files. I keep my set over here in the (inaudible) . . . Here we are.

CASE: Is this the material dating from his high school, er . . . disturbance?

SOKOLOW: If you mean by that, when I first treated him as a disturbed personality, yes.

CASE: We've requested this information through the Board of Ed. They haven't been able to locate their folder.

SOKOLOW: Not surprising, considering the state of efficiency of most municipal agencies.

CASE: That's not what I meant. Their file was removed.

SOKOLOW: By whom?

CASE: We don't know.

SOKOLOW: Then it was stolen. And you think by Eddie. Is that it?

CASE: Yes, Doctor, we do. All background data on Mr. Rodriguez seems to have disappeared as completely as he has. Did I say something funny?

SOKOLOW: No, no. You must excuse me. It's just the thought of a nineteen-year-old managing to remove all his records from at least three major agencies without being detected . . .

CASE: The Agency doesn't find it amusing, Doctor.

SOKOLOW: Agencies never do. Perhaps a bit more humor would make for a better agency, don't you think?

CASE: I don't make the Agency policy, Doctor. I only follow orders.

SOKOLOW: Ah, that takes me back to my childhood. But you know all about that, don't you? I'm sure you investigated me long before you called me, correct?

CASE: Yes, we did.

SOKOLOW: Now we are getting somewhere, Mr. Case. And though I realize that I shall never have the truth from you about the real purpose of this investigation, I feel a bit better volunteering this information. You would have gotten it by other means in any event.

CASE: Frankly, ma'am, I don't know.

SOKOLOW: Mr. Case, have you noticed that every time you lie to me, you preface your statement with how sincere you are? As a professional investigator dealing with another equally professional investigator, I'd suggest that you improve your technique. No matter. No, please don't protest. It reinforces the fault. Let's not fence any further. Forgive me if I read to you from the file. I'm afraid that my handwriting leaves much to be desired. And, of course, a good deal of it is in German.

CASE: I read and write German.

SOKOLOW: Of course you do. I should have realized that all tax investigators do. . . . (reading) I first encountered Eduardo Rodriguez while engaged in New York Municipal Project UPLIFT. You are familiar with this project, Mr. Case?

6

CASE: I'm afraid not, ma'am.

SOKOLOW: A pity. It was cancelled for lack of funds by your federal government last year. Quite simply, the project was one of retesting. You see, the so-called IQ tests are completely unreliable, even as indicators in minority testing. They are all predicated on comprehension of the English language.

CASE: I see.

SOKOLOW: I don't think you do. They are unreliable for Spanish-speaking children, naturally. But they are also culturally unsound. They ask questions about places and things that an underprivileged child would never encounter. They also are worded in a style of English that some Blacks whose native language is English cannot cope with. As the old mathematical saw goes: you can't divide apples into oranges. UPLIFT was an attempt to do culturally valid testing. We felt that we were missing potentially valuable members of society because we were asking them the wrong questions.

CASE: And Eddie Rodriguez? How did he score on these new tests?

SOKOLOW: You're all business, aren't you? Eddie scored so high, we couldn't accurately compute his level.

CASE: Which is why you saw him?

SOKOLOW: No. I didn't see him until he had undergone a whole new series of tests, some of which he had already taken some years before. The testing staff was puzzled. He had run off results infinitely superior on the second time around.

CASE: Superior in what respect?

SOKOLOW: In every respect. By the standards of the new tests and the so-called IQ tests, Eddie had become what laymen refer to as a genius, whatever

7

that term may mean. But at the same time, he was failing in all subjects in his high school curriculum and was within inches of being expelled from school for his antisocial behavior pattern.

CASE: Antisocial?

SOKOLOW: Perhaps not the proper term. Eddie was definitely social. He was the acknowledged leader of a street gang called the Barons. The group under Eddie's leadership had been suspected of a series of car thefts and burglaries so well planned and executed that no legal action could be brought against them. They were also controlling neighborhood activities in what is usually the province of organized crime in the ghetto area: lottery numbers, lesser narcotic sales, some teen-age prostitution.

CASE: Sounds like quite a boy. Are you certain there wasn't any outside help in the planning?

SOKOLOW: So far as local law enforcement could tell, no.

CASE: And was it actually Eddie who planned these things?

SOKOLOW: That's privileged information again, Mr. Case. . . . Oh, I don't mind telling you. There was no way he could have been convicted then, or now. Yes, he did. He planned it all. He used sixty-two teen-agers as a general would an army. He reorganized the whole gang along paramilitary lines. Loyalty and discipline were absolute. I'm sure you can appreciate that sort of efficiency at the, um . . . Tax Bureau, Mr. Case?

CASE: Are you baiting me, Dr. Sokolow?

SOKOLOW: Let's say, ah . . . what is the term? Twitting. Yes, I am twitting you. In any event, all such activities ceased about six weeks after he began therapy.

8

CASE: And how long did he remain in therapy?

SOKOLOW: Seven weeks.

CASE: Why did he discontinue therapy?

SOKOLOW: He didn't. I did.

CASE: For what reason, may I ask?

SOKOLOW: You may, indeed. I'll even answer that one. I discontinued therapy for the best reason an analyst can have. There was no longer a need for my services.

CASE: You mean he was cured in seven weeks?

SOKOLOW: What is cured? He was never ill to begin with. He was merely being the best survivor in his own social element. That which we term immoral in our society is perfectly acceptable behavior in others—in some cases, in societies which coexist with ours, what some call "sub-cultures." In Eddie's case, it became simply a redirection of energies into more acceptable channels. Acceptable to more of the people outside the ghetto, that is.

CASE: And so he went forth and sinned no more, eh?

SOKOLOW: That's from your Testament, not mine, Mr. Case. So far as Eddie was concerned, he had never sinned to begin with. In his particular milieu, the only real sin was getting caught. So different from your government, yes?

CASE: I wouldn't know.

SOKOLOW: Again, a pity. In any event, he shortly changed his goals. He turned the Barons into a force in the community for social change: civil rights demonstrations, parole and probation reform, day care centers, and the eradication of drugs and street crime from the *barrio*.

CASE: Yes, we have a file on the Barons.

SOKOLOW: I thought you might. Any time a force

for reform comes from *within*, authority feels there is outside leadership from . . . what is the current term? . . . subversive elements. But I forget. You don't investigate subversives at the Tax Bureau, do you?

CASE: No, Doctor, we don't.

SOKOLOW: Hew very comforting. I thought perhaps (interruption: not audible) . . . Oh yes. Good evening, Joanne. Can you wait just a few minutes out in the foyer? (inaudible response) . . . You must excuse me, Mr. Case. I have a rather busy schedule.

CASE: Certainly, Doctor. Just a few direct questions, if I may. Can you give us a physical description of Mr. Rodriguez?

SOKOLOW: As of two years ago, yes. (reading) Five feet, seven inches tall. Weight: one hundred thirty-five pounds. Hair and eyes: dark brown. Medium olive complexion . . . Do you want the results of the physical examination and tests I did?

CASE: Is that a usual procedure? A physical, I mean?

SOKOLOW: No, and a great pity. Too often we psychiatrists are called in to treat emotional problems that have physical origins—hormonal imbalance, hearing and visual problems. It's my usual procedure to have a complete physical examination, blood chemistry, and basal metabolism tests done. The full report is here if you wish to see it.

CASE: Only if there are any distinguishing marks or characteristics that would be of help in identification. You know, scars, birth defects or marks, dental work.

SOKOLOW: None whatever. He hadn't so much as a blemish or even a decayed tooth the last time I saw him. He was in perfect health. And by that I do mean complaint-free. He was the healthiest, most perfect physical specimen I have ever seen. Of course, he may be much changed in appearance by now.

CASE: What do you mean?

SOKOLOW: Well, he is still an adolescent. He may be taller, have gained weight. Hair color and texture are subject to change as is complexion tone.

CASE: And you say you have spoken to him on the telephone since then?

SOKOLOW: Yes, I have. He calls me.

CASE: From where?

SOKOLOW: I don't know. I never ask.

CASE: And what do you talk about?

SOKOLOW: I'm sorry, that is privileged doctor-patient information.

CASE: I thought you said that you had discontinued therapy with Mr. Rodriguez.

SOKOLOW: I have.

CASE: Then how can it be privileged, if he is no longer in analysis?

SOKOLOW: I didn't say I was treating him.

CASE: Well, obviously he can't be treating you.

SOKOLOW: That's the trouble with you Tax Bureau chaps. You are so intent on your little intrigues, you often miss the obvious.

CASE: What do you mean, Doctor?

SOKOLOW: I mean exactly what I say, Mr. Case. You should try directness sometime as a way of expression. You may find it refreshing, if not outright comforting. Now you must excuse me. My patient has been waiting some time, now.

CASE: Of course. Thank you, Dr. Sokolow. You've been a great help.

SOKOLOW: Have I? I'm glad. It's the purpose of my life, you know. Good evening, Mr. Case.

CASE: Good evening, Doctor. I suppose you won't

call me at the number on my card if you should hear from Eddie?

SOKOLOW: No more than I may suppose that my telephone is not being monitored. Good evining, Mr. Case.

(END TRANSCRIPT)

P.S. Hey, Hensk, bear in mind what I said about sending a Spanish-speaking agent to talk to Guzman. Guzman comes from a different culture. I can only guess at what he thought of me and the cover story I gave him. *G.T.C.*

RAFAEL GUZMAN

That cop was around again looking for Eddie Rodriguez. I didn't say anything, naturally. You'd think after a while, the dude would get the message. Nobody in this neighborhood talks to cops. Least of all, this kid. To make it worse, the dude keeps saying he's not a cop. Sure, he's looking for Eddie to give him a lot of bread. I don't know what they teach those clowns in cop school about us people up here. They think we fall down and kiss their feet for a few lousy bucks.

And the clothes on this guy! I never in my life seen a dude could make a leisure suit look like a uniform, but this one manages. All he needs is a big electric sign that says COP. I feel funny even talking to him. Someone would see and figure me for a fink. But then again, I gotta talk to him when he comes up to me on the street where I work. See, I got this fruit store on Madison and 113th Street with my brother. And this cop always buys something when he comes around.

But I don't figure him for a city cop. Too square. A city cop would just flash the tin. And not buy anything. My guess is that this dude is a Fed. I don't know what Eddie got into, but somebody wants him. Real bad.

It doesn't really surprise me, though. I always knew Eddie would wind up doing something big, good or bad. He was that kind of kid. We go back a long way, Eddie and me. We went to PS 324 together, and high school, too. Altogether, I know Eddie seven, eight years.

But the truth is, I ain't seen Eddie since six months ago. I hear from him once in awhile. He sends me a card, always from different places. I saved them, too. I got them in a box upstairs from the store, where I live. You can think that's funny, but not to me. See, if it wasn't for Eddie, me and my brother, Pablo, wouldn't have this store. The last time I saw Eddie, he gave me and Pablo the bread to get started. And I don't mean loaned it to us. It was a gift, man.

He came around one afternoon when he knew I'd be working at the store. Greenberg owned it then, and me and Pablo was just clerks and delivery boys. I was emptying some sacks of potatoes into a bin and I hear someone say, "Rafael, *¿qué tal?*" I look up, and there's Eddie.

At first, I almost didn't know him. I took him for some downtown *gringo*. He was wearing a suit with a vest, and he looked like those dudes you see in the ads in *Playboy*. Right at the curb is a new Mercedes-Benz convert with the top down. A bunch of the neighborhood kids was starting to come around just to dig it. He was drawing a crowd like he was the head *chulo* in the *barrio* inspecting the troops.

One of the kids starts in on him with the watch-the-car riff. That's where the kids ask for money to watch your car. What they really mean is, you don't pay them something, they rip you off for everything in the car when you walk away. Or if you ain't got anything in there, they do up your tires and top.

They seen Eddie's clothes and the car and figured just what I did. They even was talking to Eddie in English. Now, when this happens, you got two ways to go. You can pay, which makes you a sucker. Or you can hardnose the kids and take your chances, which makes you a sucker because they'll screw up your car. What Eddie did is what makes him Eddie.

He calls over the biggest kid and asks him in Spanish, "You, kid. What's your name?"

The kid hesitates and says, "Rafael Garcia."

Eddie gives him a big smile and says, "No, it isn't. You're Lydia Prieto's kid brother, Paco. You live across the street. Fifth floor, in back." Then he takes a half a buck from his pocket. "You see this, Paco?" he says, holding it up. The kid just nods and gives him a "all-right-you-caught-me" grin.

Then, between his thumb and first finger, Eddie bends the half-a-buck coin like it was made of clay. He hands it to Paco and says, "Paco, me and my man Rafael here are going down the block to Chuchi's Bar and talk. When we come back, if there's so much as a scratch on this car, I'm gonna bend you just as good as that fifty cents. Don't forget. I know where you live. But if the car is all right, and if somebody wipes it down and keeps the other kids away, you get the other half of this."

14

Then he takes out a roll of bills and peels off a five, tears it in half, and hands it to Paco.

That's what I mean about Eddie. He's got the kid the same two ways the kid was trying to get him. I seen the kid looking hard at the half a buck and trying to see if it was a trick Eddie did with it. But it wasn't any trick, man. Eddie really bent the sucker with two fingers. Hell, if he did that with me and we wasn't tight, I would have watched his car till next year. And forget the five bucks.

It wasn't until we were sitting in a booth at Chuchi's that I remembered. The Prietos had only lived on the block for a few months. I know, I'd been trying to get next to Lydia since they moved in. Now how the hell could Eddie have known the kid, where he lived and Lydia too? I looked across the booth at Eddie. It was hard to believe it was the same guy I went to PS 324 and most of high school with. He was the same, but somehow different. No one big difference, just a lot of little ones.

Like his front teeth. When we first met, his two upper front teeth overlapped just a little. And the one on the right had a chip in it. I remember how it happened. We went to war with *Los Tigres* one spring, and he got rapped in the mouth with a stick. But now, he looked like a toothpaste commercial. Well, if you got the bread, you can get your teeth fixed up, I guess.

Not only the teeth were different. Eddie was taller and wider than I remember. But when you don't see somebody for a long time, your memory can play tricks. Besides, they say you keep growing until you're in your twenties. I figured that was it. But the weirdest thing was his eyes. I swear to God they were lighter in color. I know for a fact that me and

Eddie has the same color eyes. When we were little, everybody used to take us for brothers. That's how much alike we were. I asked him about it. He laughed.

"Contact lenses, Rafael. They change the color in certain kinds of light."

"When did you start wearing glasses?" I asked. "You always had the best eyesight of anyone in the gang."

"In college. I was studying my tail off, trying to keep up with all those rich kids."

It figured. I know Eddie. He had to win. He wouldn't want to just keep up, though. He'd want to be the best. Letting it pass, I started filling him in on all the things that had gone down in the time since we last rapped together. I told him how I'd been working with my brother Pablo for Greenberg at the fruit store. And how Greenberg was sick and wanted to get out. I don't think Greenberg was really sick, though. Just tired.

See, when Greenberg first opened up the store, the neighborhood was mostly Italian. Greenberg speaks Italian pretty good. I hear him with his old customers.

When I asked the old man about it, he explained that he had to learn Italian to stay in business. I asked him how come he didn't learn Spanish now, instead of having me and Pablo wait on the *Latino* customers, which is almost everybody. He said he was too old and he was tired. That's when he first said that if anybody offered him a fair price, he'd sell out in a flash and retire to Florida. Eddie stopped me right there.

"What does Greenberg think is fair, Rafael?" I told him the figure and he said, "Uh-huh." I went on telling him how things on the block had changed. In a few minutes, I realized I was doing all the talking. I didn't know any more about what Eddie'd been doing than I did when we started. It didn't used to be that way. Me and Eddie would get together and talk about all the great things we was going to do when we got a few coins together.

What a laugh. Once my old man had the stroke, I had to drop out of school and work with Pablo for Greenberg. And I was lucky to get the job. Try getting a decent job in this town without being a high school graduate, let alone being a *Latino*. And looking it, too. Not that Greenberg was breaking his heart with what he pays me and Pablo. But I can count as good as anyone. I saw how much the store made. My whole family could live all right on it. Pablo could even afford to marry that *gringa* downtown that he keeps taking out.

But like I told Eddie, it was all a dream. If my brother and me saved everything we made, we could maybe make enough for a down payment after a year. But in the meantime, we couldn't afford to eat. That's how the *barrio* gets you, babe. All around you, in magazine ads and on TV, you see the things you can't get. So you get into the buying on credit. You can't buy the good goods; they don't sell them on time payments uptown. So you end up with stuff that falls apart. But the payments don't stop. Before you know it, you got a chain around your neck. And you never get loose. I saw my old man work two, three jobs just to meet the payments. What did it get him but a heart attack? Now me and Pablo are busting our backs to make the payments. The same ones he couldn't keep up.

But what the hell, I told Eddie. At least we got

jobs until Greenberg dies or sells out. And the color TV is still working. Papa would go crazy if he couldn't watch it. He can't move around. I looked at Eddie, and I stopped talking. I swear to God he was crying. I never seen Eddie Rodriguez cry. Ever. Not even the time they took the stitches in his arm the night that dude cut him. I asked him what was wrong.

"The contact lenses," he says. "Must be the smoke in here." He leaned over the table and passed his hand in front of his eyes. He made like he was putting something in his pocket, and when he looked at me again, his eyes were clear. And the same color as mine.

Now, I don't want to call my main man a liar, but I know if you wear contacts, you got to put them in a little case when you take them out. Otherwise, you screw them up. I didn't say nothing, though.

Eddie looked at me for a second, real hard. Then he smiles real big. "Rafael," he says, like he knew what I was thinking, "you're right. A lot of things have happened to me since we last met. I'm living a different life. I got out. It's a whole other world. I'm not sure I can deal with it. Not the way I want to, anyway." He shook his head, like he was clearing it. "But that's my thing. I want to talk to you about your thing. And I need a favor from you."

"From me? What can I do for a dude with a pocketful of money and a Mercedes convert? Polish your car?"

Eddie laughed. "No, I got a kid outside that's wiping it down right now. I want you to buy something for me."

Now, this, I can understand. Lots of guys in the rackets uptown have friends buy things for them. See, they make a lot of money, but the Man is always watching them. Soon as they start spending too much bread, the Feds close in and ask questions about where the bread is coming from.

Eddie saw my smile and waved a finger at me. "No, no. My man, this is going to be clean money."

He calls Chuchi over to the booth and has him bring another round and a copy of the *New York Post*. He turns right away to the racing page and looks over the lines for the trotters at all the New York tracks for that night. Then he takes out a leather-bound notebook and a gold pen and starts writing. In a few minutes, he has two full pages of numbers and names written down. He hands it to me and says, "Rafael, I want you to go to all the OTB offices I've written down here. Play these combinations *exactly* as I have them here. I want you to double up your bets only where I say to. There are three losers on the slip. Bet them, too, but the way I say. If you don't there'll be a stink at the tracks and they'll hold up payments on you and investigate."

"I get it. I can't look too good. Right?"

"Right. Take this money. The way I have it laid out, by tomorrow, you'll have enough to buy the store and the building from Greenberg. The money left over is for taxes on what you're going to win. Don't touch any of the money over the price of the business and the building. That's for Uncle Sam. If you do, the Feds will come and take away what you got, *comprendes*?"

"Got it."

"OK. And this is for some decent stuff for the apartment." He reaches into another pocket and takes out still more cash. "I only want one thing from you in return," he says.

I looked at him and said, "Who do you want

killed?" I don't know even now if I was kidding or not. You can't know what it means when you just about give up hope for anything, to have someone give it back to you.

"That's my main man," says Eddie, smiling. "But all I want you to do is what you wanted to do. Buy the building and the business. I don't want you to go crazy when you see the money and piss it all away."

"I swear to God, Eddie."

"No, not to God. On your word as *un hombre de honor* and as a Baron."

I felt like the kid that Eddie had got two ways on the street, about the car. He was asking me the toughest oath you can ask. My word as a man of honor, and you have to understand what honor means to a *Latino*, and my word as a member of the Barons, our gang. To break either word, you'd have to kill me first. I swallowed hard, gave him the secret grip, and promised. I promised more than that, too.

I swore that when I bought the store from Greenberg, that I wouldn't rent the apartment upstairs where Greenberg lived. I was to buy some cheap furniture, some canned groceries, and change all the locks on the doors and window bars. I knew what this was about. Eddie was into something heavy and wanted a place where no one could find him if he hid out. Pretty smart. Greenberg had bars and a steel door. Nobody could crash into that place.

We finished our drinks and walked back to where Paco Prieto was standing in the same spot by the Mercedes. The car didn't have a speck of dust on it, and everything was where it was when we left.

Eddie gave the kid the other half of the five, and Paco took off.

We rapped awhile longer in front of the store. Pablo came out, and we played remember when for a few minutes. But really, Pablo and Eddie was never tight. It was more polite than anything else. Greenberg stayed in the store. We were speaking Spanish, so he didn't bother to come out. We promised to see each other again soon, and then Eddie got in the car and drove off.

I watched him go and went into the store to tell Greenberg I had some outside business to do today, meaning what Eddie told me. Then I realized Eddie hadn't told me where to send the keys for the new locks on Greenberg's pad. I ran down to the corner and looked for the car. I thought I saw it at a red light up the block. I swear it was the same car. You don't see that many of them up here. But the dude driving was real light and blond-haired. And that was the last time I seen Eddie Rodriguez.

FOLLOW-UP REPORT: EYES ONLY

To: District Supervisor Darryl Henskey

From: Field Agent G.T. Case

Dear Hensk,

This is over and above the regular report. What the hell is going on? I can't do the job if you keep me on a "need-to-know" basis. I thought we were dealing with a new kind of securities swindle that had international overtones. I further thought that this Rodriguez kid was the cat's-paw for some organization, domestic and/or foreign.

It's starting to look like the kid was doing it all himself. I know that's crazy, but nothing about this investigation is ordinary. I keep telling myself that no kid, regardless of the books he's read, could have pulled off the stunt you described to me. But now, I wonder. It seems he's not only absorbed the teaching at the university, but somehow, some way, he's extracted the total experience of the faculty, the same way you'd squeeze an orange for the juice.

I disagree with you that the kid is a plant. Sure, the disappearing records point in that direction. But I'm satisfied that we are dealing with the same Eddie Rodriguez born in New York City. There are too many overlaps to justify thinking there was a substitution anywhere along the line.

Here's a hot flash for you. Our physical descriptions don't jibe. Oh, all the basics are there. It could be that the kid just grew five inches taller. Kids have done that in a year's time. But it seems to have all come in one spurt, shortly after he arrived at Midwestern. Being an athlete, his measurements and condition are matters of record. I'm enclosing a stat. If you look at the figures from the September arrival and then the figures for the start of the second semester, you'll see what I mean. I checked with the coach of the track team. The spurt of growth coincided almost exactly with Rodriguez's poor early showing in hurdles. The coach was going to keep him on sprints and relays because of it. It had to do with his height. Just not tall enough for hurdles. But by the time spring track meets came up, hocus-pocus, he's tall enough. Spooky, huh?

Listen, Hensk, there's something going on here. I'm no longer satisfied with that Sokolow interview. I also would like you to get a Spanish-speaking operative to re-interview Rodriguez's sister. The hell of it is that I can't tell you exactly what I'm looking for. I also get the feeling that you're holding back a lot that could help me put it all together. I'd like to meet with you after I recheck New York. Please have that Spanish-speaking agent on call for me when I get to Fun City, OK?

Best,

George

MIDWESTERN UNIVERSITY INTERVIEWS

Henry Bradley

Gee, Mr. Case, I wish I could tell you a lot about Eddie, but I just can't. We were roommates for a year, but I couldn't say I really knew him. He didn't hang with the rest of the guys on the track team.

I thought at first it was because of him being Puerto Rican, he wanted to be alone. No, I don't mean he wanted to be alone just for that. I mean he would of wanted to be alone because there wasn't anyone else like him around. There's lots of guys go here don't think a lot of anyone with a Spanish accent. Yeah, I know it's silly, but that happens to be where they're at. I look at it like it's their problem.

Anyway, it's funny you should ask about Eddie. That was one strange kid. I really mean it. You

23

know, I never saw him sleep? No kidding, I don't think he ever slept. He was always up and dressed before I was, and when I'd go to sleep at night, he was still up reading or studying. That's another funny thing. We're all of us in this wing on athletic scholarships. And to tell the truth, they don't really ask much more of us than not to screw up at the meets. I mean, we don't have to be geniuses or anything. But not Eddie. He was carrying twelve credits in heavy stuff, too. I mean, none of this underwater basket weaving crap.

You'd think that a guy who was averaging B pluses to A's would be a drag to room with, but he wasn't. He was a regular guy. We used to laugh a lot. Sometimes he used to talk about where he came from. I mean in New York. No, Eddie wasn't born in Puerto Rico. Just his mom and dad. Anyway, he used to tell me about his neighborhood and the people on his block like it was a small town. It was like reading a book, hearing him talk. I think if I ever went to his block, I'd know everyone there by sight, just the way he told me they'd be.

But the funny thing, with all the talking about his neighborhood, I never really got much from him about himself. You know, some guys have ideas about what they'd like to do. Like, I know I'm going to end up teaching Phys. Ed. But inside, what I'd really like to have a shot at is being a car mechanic. I don't mean like the guy at the gas station. I mean to work on really great cars, modified and full-race. But I know how it's going to end up. Everybody's got a dream, right? Not Eddie. Or if he did, he never said zip about it.

I'll tell you one thing, though. On the field, that guy could do anything. Hundred meters, 400 hurdles, steeplechase, name it. And he used to drive Coach crazy. See, he never looked like he was trying. Not a hundred percent, anyway. That's Coach's war cry: one hunnndred percent, dammit, one hunnndred per goddamn cent! You get the idea.

Anyway, Eddie would always turn in the winning times. It was spooky. Whatever it took to win, no more, no less. If the field was slow, Eddie was just a little faster. If we were up against a tough team, he'd be even tougher. One meet, I saw him do a hundred yards in 8.7, and that's a record. It was unofficial, naturally, but once Coach saw he could do it, he wanted more. But you can't blame Coach, either. I mean, his job would be golden for years if we could send a man to the Olympics.

But he couldn't move Eddie any faster than Eddie wanted to go. I heard some locker room sessions with Coach and Eddie. As much as Coach would holler and chew him out, that's how quiet Eddie would get. The upshot of it was that Eddie won. Hell, Coach couldn't bounce him. He was the best guy we had. All Eddie would ever say when Coach started in giving the needle was, "We won, didn't we?" And you got to admit he was right.

Oh, hey, I almost forgot. You ought to talk to Artie Ramos. He's not on the team. He's regular matric. He's from Spain. His old man teaches romance languages here. Eddie used to go talk Spanish with him and his father. How the hell should I know what they talked about? It wouldn't matter. I didn't take Spanish. Just French, and never more than a C. Hey, that's all right. I was glad to help you.

Oh, by the way, Mr. Case. Does the Bureau pay well? I mean, I was thinking, it would be swift doing what you do. I mean, going around the country and investigating things. Tell me, do you need a lot of math for your job? Oh, too bad.

Arturo Ramos, Sr.

Quite simply, sir, the boy is a genius. Not a lopsided adept in some aspect of scholastic pursuit. His is the true genius. All languages are as one to him after a few hours. His grasp of the root of any matter is uncanny. When I first saw him at work, I was convinced he had stumbled upon some new method of learning languages. But as near as I can determine, he is the ultimate conceptual thinker. He is capable of finding the basis of any problem, relating it to experience, no matter how tenuous the thread, then weaving threads into cables of steel-clad logic. I simply cannot understand why the boy was here on an athletic scholarship. He could have won a scholastic allowance, not really equal to the amount he received as an athlete, but adequate. Every time I mentioned this, he would remind me of *mens sana*. As I say, irrefutable logic.

As to how he maintained his studies and athletic pursuits, your question is easily answered. The boy did not sleep. No, that's not as unusual as you might think. There are people in this world who do not sleep. They are something of an enigma. And they manifest no ill effects from it, either. They just do not sleep. Ah, sometimes I envy them! What must it be like to not leave a third of one's life behind, unused? But I must confess that nothing really makes me feel better than a good dinner, the right wine, a fine cigar, and a good night's sleep. Perhaps

I'm growing older. There was a time when I would not have been so satisfied if there were nothing between cigar and sleep.

But you wish to know more about Eduardo, I can tell you everything and yet, nothing. He read everything, he assimilated it, then went on. He came to me because he felt his Spanish was inadequate. He was quite right, of course. He spoke what we call "Spanglish." Atrocious accent, riddled with constructions and words that pertain to English more than Spanish. It's an argot, really. Do you know that within six weeks, his Spanish was flawless? And he still retained complete mastery and accent of his argot as well. What it meant to me was that he'd acquired Spanish as a foreign language. Foreign from his argot, that is.

What astounded me was that while in the process of learning proper Spanish, he was simultaneously acquiring French, Italian, Portuguese, and Romanian!

It was at this time I became convinced I had come upon a major educational discovery. I wanted to bring him to the attention of the entire faculty. But, of course, I couldn't. He didn't want me to do it.

Draw attention to his grades? Nonsense. He was only registered for one language: Spanish. In it, his grades were excellent. However, one cannot approach a faculty meeting on the basis of excellent grades in Spanish, particularly if the student in question is Hispanic to begin with. There was no way I could force him to display his knowledge. In the end, I abandoned the idea.

However, this may be of interest to you. When Eduardo left so abruptly, I spoke to some of my colleagues about him. To a man, they had all shared my experience with Eduardo, each in his own specialty! The only instructor who didn't share my enthusiasm about Eduardo's talents was Bloch of the mathematics department. He'd had words with young Rodriguez about something to do with an aspect of higher mathematics. As to what it might have been, I couldn't say. Frankly, higher mathematics has always eluded me. Bloch explained to me what it was, but I still don't understand. Brilliant man, Bloch, but no educator.

Delighted to have been of some assistance. I hope you find Eduardo well and happy. I worry about him. But now, knowing that an official inquiry is in the process, I feel better. They say you chaps always get your man. Or is that the Royal Canadian Mounted Police? In any event, good hunting!

Arturo Ramos, Jr.

No, sir. He wasn't my friend, exactly. I'd say he was more friendly with my father. In all the time I knew Eddie, I had the feeling that he was inside himself. That he was only letting me, or anyone, see what he wanted us to see.

Oh, we went places together. Movies, mostly, and only old ones. You know the classic films programs that they run at The Art in town? They change the program once a week, on Thursdays. Every Thursday, we'd eat at the Pizza Shack or MacDonald's, see the "new" old movie and then go to my house. Eddie would start talking with my father, then. I just kind of sat around. After a few Thursdays like that, I got the hint, and I used to take off once they got wound up.

Girls? Sure, Eddie was straight that way. But no, I never heard him mention anyone specific. No, he never dated any of the girls at school. But twice a month, he used to go into Chicago. Alone. He never said where, exactly. I get the feeling he headed for the Latin ghetto area. He used to say once in awhile that he had to check out his roots. I assumed by his roots he meant the company of others with . . . er, similar backgrounds, shall we say? You're right. I don't know for sure. I guess it was the way he said he was going to Chicago that led me to think it.

Glad to have been of help, sir. And if you find Eddie, say hello for me, will you? In a strange way, I miss him a great deal. So does Professor Cass. He was talking to my father the other day about Eddie. Professor Cass plays chess with my dad twice a week. What does he teach? Economics. He's the chairman of the department. Sure, you're welcome.

Ellsworth Cass

Fantastic mind, simply fantastic. Miss him? Of course I do. He was a breath of air. A true inquiring mind. Odd, isn't it? You'd think that a university would be the first place you'd find such a mind. But it isn't. We've become a system of vocational schools that don't really teach vocations. Your average student here is concerned with grades. Grades mean averages, averages mean honors. Honors mean a better, more highly paid job after graduation.

But Eddie. What a pleasure! He was only a freshman, and I was surprised when he came to me. First-year students get a survey course in Economics. It's required. But he'd already gone well beyond the scope of any survey when he asked for an appointment with me. I checked with his instructor and found he was at the top of his class. And he wanted to know more.

Mr. Case, I have a theory about students. Once in a great while, a potentially excellent mind comes your way. You then have a responsibility to that mind as a teacher. You can spot them, too. They send up little flares, if you know what to look for. In Eddie's case, he wanted to know about Keynes. To me, that was a flare. I gave him all and any information he wanted.

The market? Which market? Oh, the exchanges. Certainly, we discussed the market. But not to the exclusion of any other aspect of my specialty. Eddie wasn't interested in any one small facet of Economics. He wanted to know it all. I was delighted. Mr. Case, you can't know how few youngsters today show both aptitude and inclination for the study of Economics. That's why I was disappointed when he left us so abruptly. I was hoping he would have elected for a career in the field. I wrote to his sister in New York, asking after him, but we never received a reply. We? Professor Ramos and myself. The sister doesn't speak that much English. Arthur wrote the letter in Spanish. The address? Yes, I'm sure I have it here, somewhere.

You're perfectly welcome. By the way, would you clarify something for me? I don't understand why your agency should be interested in a missing-persons' case. I thought you were in charge of things like kidnappings. Do you think something has happened to Eddie? Oh, I see. Do you often work on only one aspect of a case? How interesting. Then your supervisor must put all the reports together like a jigsaw puzzle. Could I write to him and find out? Well, I'd like to try, anyway. Just care of the address on your card, eh? Very well. And good day to you, too.

INTERIM REPORT: EYES ONLY

To: Field Agent G.T. Case
From: Operative J.B. Ortiz
Re: Interview with Aida Ruiz (nee Rodriguez)

Dear Mr. Case,

I am enclosing both the verbatim and interpretive translations of Mrs. Ruiz's interview. I'd suggest you follow the interpretive. A lot of the verbatim is misleading because of her manner of speaking. She's a member of a small, fundamentalist church. Her entire life is centered around her church activities. It seems that both her parents were killed in a tenement fire, her brother fell near fatally ill, and her husband abandoned her and her newborn child, so she turned to the church for strength and comfort. She's been a mainstay of the church ever since.

The text of the interview would seem to be the ravings of a deranged person if one were not aware of her background. I believe her to be sane. I also believe that she is telling the letter of the truth as she sees it. She firmly believes she'd burn in hell if she lied. If she withheld anything, it would only have been that I didn't know enough to ask her. I proceeded strictly along the lines of the interview pattern you drafted.

I found the subject at her home and at the address you provided. She has lived there for the past two years. In terms of the neighborhood, it is a "good" building. Well-maintained. Her apartment and furnishings all in keeping with her income. Her child (son Luis) is bright and personable and appears healthy, happy, and normal in all respects.

I would estimate subject's age as closer to thirty than the twenty-two years you indicate. Physical description otherwise one hundred percent. She is small, with dark hair and eyes, and a medium-olive complexion. She gives off a feeling of peace and serenity in her conversation on all subjects except her brother, Eduardo. But you can read that attitude for yourself.

If any of the finer points of the translation need clarification, don't hesitate to call me at home. The number's in my persfile.

Sincerely,

J.B. Ortiz

AIDA RUIZ

I have no brother. My brother died four years ago in Lenox Hill Hospital. He had brain fever and he died. The person you call Eduardo Rodriguez is not my brother. I know he has the same body, the same voice. But something evil has his soul. A devil!

I thought at first, when he came home from the

hospital, that he had had a divine vision; that he had spoken with saints or perhaps God. Did you know that when he lay in fever in the hospital, he spoke in tongues? It's true. I was there at his bedside, through the night. At first, he mumbled. But then as I listened, he began to speak in languages I never heard. No, you can tell the difference when someone raves and someone speaks a language. It has a . . . rhythm to it.

One of the nurses, she was from somewhere far away—India, I think—said he was speaking in her language. That is a sign of visitation, you know, speaking in languages you have never heard.

I prayed for him. God forgive me, I prayed for his life. Two other children in the neighborhood had already died of this brain fever.* The doctors said that my prayers would do as much as *they* could. I thought that my prayers were being answered! For when I spoke to him, prayed for him, he answered.

He quoted the Bible as he lay there, almost dead of the fever. I remember I was reading from the Psalms. It was a psalm of David that has always comforted me since my parents died. It goes: *When my father and mother forsake me, then the Lord will take me up.*

And from the bed, as though he were wide awake, not near death, I heard Eduardo continue: *Teach me thy way, O Lord, and lead me in a plain path because of my enemies.*

Now, I know that Eduardo had never read this psalm. Eduardo never read any psalms. The little he had read of the Bible was at my insistence. When-

---

*This story checks out with an outbreak of meningitis in the city about that time. *J.B.O.*

ever he would be in trouble, I would make him read those verses that would help him. But outside of that, he never opened the book.

The long night passed, and he recovered from the fever. I thanked God daily for sparing the last of my family. And I promised God that the life he had spared would be spent in good works and repentance. But once he was home and recovered, I could not keep my promise, may God forgive me.

Eduardo did not go to church, but when I took him. He always preferred to sleep late on Sundays. He would spend his Saturdays and nights with that trash, the Barons. Sleep? Of course he slept. He was lazy. He could sleep anywhere, anytime. I, God help me, am denied that pleasure. I spend my nights tossing and turning. I listen to the breathing of my son. I listen for sounds that might mean trouble, robbers, fire. My sleep is always troubled. It has been since my mother and father died in a fire. My father saved Eduardo and me. He died when he went back for my mother, and the building floor collapsed. And Eduardo? He fell asleep in my arms as I stood on the sidewalk holding him.

But after he returned from the hospital, things got even worse. He went wild. Suddenly, there were comings and goings at our apartment late at night. As I say, I sleep fitfully. Members of the Barons would climb the fire escape and go into Eduardo's room. I heard them talking, and my heart cried out in me, for the things they spoke of were evil! I recall one night when Guzman came. Rafael Guzman. The brother Pablo is a good man. He goes to church and works hard. Rafael was Eduardo's right hand in the Barons. Before Eduardo was sick, Rafael had been the *jefe*. But now, I could hear Eduardo

34

telling Guzman what to do. And Guzman agreeing as though Eduardo were not so much smaller and younger than he. I heard them clearly, and they spoke of their "business."

Do you know what this business was? They were stealing. They would go downtown to the rich neighborhoods and enter buildings and steal. Eduardo would somehow know where everything was in these buildings. Guzman and the others would follow Eduardo's orders and take only what he told them to take. And that's not the worst of it. They were selling drugs, they were running a *bolita**, and, God help them, they were sending young girls out to sell their bodies! They would meet at Eduardo's room each night, and Eduardo would give Guzman money from all their vile schemes. Guzman would then pay the other Barons.

One night, when I could stand it no more, I went into Eduardo's room after I heard Guzman leave by the window. I turned on the ceiling light, and he lay there in bed, pretending to sleep.

"Don't pretend, you devil!" I said. "I know you're awake, and I know what you're doing with those trash, the Barons."

"I don't know what you're talking about, little sister," he said.

"You'll know what I'm talking about when I call the police."

Eduardo sat up in bed, then. He knew I wasn't fooling about going to the police. He said very quietly, "You won't go to the police, Aida."

"Won't I?" I shouted. "Then watch me. I'm going downstairs to Rivera's and use their phone. I'm going to call the police!"

---

*bolita is the uptown variation of the numbers racket. *J.B.O.*

Eduardo gave me a strange smile. "Go then," he said.

I started for the door, and as God is my witness, I couldn't move! I stood there like Lot's wife, turned into a pillar of salt. It was as though my feet had become part of the floor.

"You see?" said Eduardo from the bed. "I told you you weren't going anywhere. You can't move at all, can you? No, don't try to speak. You can't do that, either. You are lucky you weren't foolish enough to talk to anyone about this before you spoke to me. Otherwise . . ."

I felt as though a hand of ice had been laid across my heart. I couldn't breathe. I wanted to cry out, but I still couldn't move. He sat there in the bed, smiling all the while. My vision began to blur, and I felt as though my soul was about to leave my body.

Then he actually laughed aloud. "Ah, little sister. You can't catch your breath, is that it? Very well, I'll let you breathe."

Released, I fell to the floor, like a toy he had thrown there. He got out of the bed and stood over me. I shrank away as he touched my shoulder.

"No, no. I won't hurt you, Aida," he said. "But you must forget this foolishness about the police. I'm not hurting anyone, really. We steal, yes, but only from the *gringos* downtown who have so much they can afford it. The *bolita* and the drugs, why we have only taken away those businesses from those outsiders who rape the people who live here."

"And the young girls, Eduardo. What of them?"

"There have always been such girls, there always will be. All I have done is to show them how and where they can make much more money. Naturally, I have given something of value to them and just as

36

naturally, they give me money in return. I have done nothing that no one else in the *barrio* would not have done, if he had the chance and the brains."

"You are wrong, Eduardito," I said. "Because we live the way we do, we are not free to break the laws of God."

"Then what are we free to do?" he said angrily. "Starve? Work ourselves to death like Rafael's father, with two and three jobs, to live in junk heaps like this with rats and roaches? Is that God's will? If it is, He's no true God!"

I wanted to scream "blasphemy" from where I lay on the floor. But again, no sound would come from my throat.

Eduardo stood there looking down at me and said, "Don't try to cry out, sister. In fact, you will find that every time you try, nothing will happen. And in the future, don't even bother. You'll find you can't talk to police or anyone else about me. Unless, of course, you want to tell them what a good and sweet brother you have. That *will* come out, no matter what you want to say."

He turned, then, and went back to bed. And may God help me, he was right. We lived together in the same apartment for the next two years. Not once was I able to speak a word against him. I thought I would go mad, living under the same roof with this creature, this devil. I saw it all happening and was powerless to do anything but pray for my soul and the soul of my son. I knew there was no hope in praying for Eduardo's soul. For that had died, I believe, long ago at the hospital.

I watched as the Barons took control of the neighborhood. I saw them go from thieves and *chulos* to workers for better things here in the *bar-*

rio. Again, it was Eduardo who planned it. But for what reason? I didn't know, but it must have been evil.

When that social worker came to the house and asked about Eduardo, I told her what I told all the others, that Eduardo was a good brother and a fine young man. She wanted to know about Eduardo's teeth. He wouldn't go to a dentist. They have a free dental plan at the high school. How could I tell her? I wanted to, but I couldn't.

A little while after he came back from the hospital, before that night when I realized he was not really Eduardo, a strange thing happened. We were having dinner and suddenly, Eduardo made a strange face and took something from his mouth and put it on his plate. I thought first: a bone. We were eating fish. But no, it was a filling from one of his teeth. I looked into his mouth to see which tooth it had come from. I found it. But there was no deep hole, the way an empty filling space would look. I know, I have had fillings fall out before.

Instead of the dark space a filling leaves, there was only a shallow place that looked like the rest of the tooth. It was then that I also noticed the upper teeth in front. Eduardo had two chipped upper teeth. He got them fighting. But now, the chip wasn't so big as before. And there was, I swear, new tooth growing, coming closer together. By the time he left for that college out west, you could hardly see any space between his teeth at all.

As to what he studied at the college, I don't know. I know nothing about Eduardo. Yes, I spoke to the Jewish lady doctor about him. What could I say? That he was a fine man and a good brother. It was the lady doctor who got the school out west for

Eduardo. She needed my permission to have him go there. I signed some papers. No, I don't know what they were. My English is not that good. The lady doctor said they were letters of permission for Eduardo to go. I signed them because Eduardo wanted me to. I did everything Eduardo wanted. I could do nothing else.

Just before Eduardo went away, the lady doctor came again to see me. She said that she had money for me. Eduardo said I must take it. I have it still. It's here in the coffee can. Yes, count it. Twelve thousand, five hundred dollars. I would not touch a cent. I could not even give it to the church. I know where it must have come from.

But it is a strange thing, Señor Ortiz. Today, I feel I could give this money away. It began only last week. I feel I can speak of Eduardo, or that devil that lives inside him. Before now, I could not. Every time I even thought of it, I felt that same feeling as I did that night when he nearly killed me. I think that now, if you find the *thing* that is Eduardo, it, too, will be as dead as my brother. I know in my heart that if that thing lived still, I would be dead on the floor before you for speaking of it.

(END INTERPRETIVE COPY)

INTERIM REPORT: PRIORITY TEN (10)

To: Field Agent G.T. Case

From: District Supervisor D. Henskey

Re: PROJECT NIETZSCHE

Dear George,

Received transcripts of new interview with Aida Ruiz. You're right. All bets off. Break off all contacts and return to HQ in Maryland immediately. For your info, prior interview with Ruiz woman yielded only that subject was "a fine man and a good brother."

I don't believe that subject is possessed by demons or dead, either. If his sister is suddenly free to talk, given what she says is true, he has simply thrown her away. He doesn't think what she has to say can hurt him anymore.

On your arrival at HQ, you will be given the full briefing you requested. I have detached Agent Ortiz from New York Area Command. In light of what he knows, he will become your No. 1. He will accompany you to Maryland.

In future, all references to subject will be under code name NIETZSCHE. New classification project: PRIORITY TEN (10). Repeat: 10. Max security observed. Will expect you earliest with Ortiz and your toothbrush.

Henskey

GEORGE T. CASE

The shuttle flight to Washington isn't crowded; it rarely is after business hours. I thought it would give me time to go over what I had in my head. But Ortiz feels talkative. Can't blame him. He's only with the Bureau a year and a half, and here he is working with the senior agent for Eastern Regional and on a Priority Ten project.

I can't help but wonder what he must think. After all, a Priority Ten is only one short of National Emergency or State of War. I guess he thinks he's saving the world as we know it. Hell, maybe we are. I won't know myself until Henskey fills me in.

This Ortiz is a nice kid. Regulation every step of the way. That's OK with me. At least I know what he'll do at any given time. Half the troubles I've gotten into in the past have been from subagents trying to improvise and "show initiative." But I can't keep my mind on Ortiz's conversation. I start thinking about the Rodriguez kid, excuse me, NIETZSCHE. Where does Henskey get these names for projects? I remember that oil assignment he christened HEARTBURN.

But NIETZSCHE. What *is* going on? I've never run across a bigger puzzle in twenty-five years with the Bureau. Every time I think a recognizable pattern is coming out, some new witness or evidence turns it all around. But I keep feeling that I'm missing something I already know. I just can't put it in place yet.

DARRYL HENSKEY

"George, Agent Ortiz . . . Joseph Ortiz, isn't it? Glad you made it as quickly as you did. All right, have a chair. Here is the NIETZSCHE file. As you can see, it's very slim. You already know most of it, George, and though I may be going over familiar ground, Agent Ortiz is almost completely in the dark. As far as data collation can go, this is the story: Just about two years ago, our securities investigation arm began to get reports on a new and private investment firm, operating out of New York, Paris, Rome, and Lisbon. Firm name was Prometheus Investments. What? Yes, *was*. Prometheus no longer exists except on paper. Please, I'd rather you hold your questions until I finish. Most of your questions will be answered as we go along.

"In any event, Prometheus started out as a regular investment firm. Just New York Exchange. They bought commodities, acted like any legit operation. The difference was that they were never wrong. I mean never. Everything Prometheus bought went up. If it went down, Prometheus was out of it at peak price. Not after, mind you. Before.

"Within a few months, the operation was large enough to begin acquiring small firms. All solid respectable corporations with a good, predictable growth curve. Then these firms suddenly began to get important government contracts. And not through registered lobbyists here in D.C.

"Values of the stock naturally went sky-high.

All well and good, so far. But then Prometheus began raiding and looting the corporations it controlled. Diverting funds to strange channels. In short, squeezing the newly acquired firms for money. They then went international and ceased dealing with anything but money and gold. It was uncanny the way that Prometheus could always predict what the rates of exchange were going to be, even on a day-to-day basis. It was at this point that we really became interested. It smelled like manipulation of the international money market. But we couldn't figure out how it was being done.

"We went to the source and tried to establish the identity of the moving force behind Prometheus. Using all the resources of the Bureau, it still took us eight weeks to get information that usually takes us a day and a half to get. We came up with four names: In France, Philippe Martel; Rome, Alberto Lugano; Lisbon, Norberto Cruz. In New York, the name was Eduardo Rodriguez.

"Starting in New York, we soon located Rodriguez. He had an apartment on Sutton Place and lived in a style befitting a man controlling a firm dealing in tens of millions. But outside of that, we couldn't get a damned thing on him. Understand, we couldn't just subpoena him or pay him a call. As far as we could see, the only thing he'd done was make a helluva lot of money. Questionably, but undoubtedly legally. And Mr. Rodriguez did not care to speak to us, period.

"We put a tail on him. He shook it. We tried women operatives. I'm sure he had a great time, but we didn't learn a thing. But what we did learn sent up flares all over the Bureau. It seems that our financial genius was an eighteen-year-old Puerto Rican kid from the New York ghetto. He'd had one year of college on an athletic scholarship at Midwestern U. No special training in finance. And get this—the initial financing for Prometheus in New York came from Rodriguez's profits at gambling here at the tracks and in Las Vegas at the casino. Oh, it was all legit. He took the terrible beating on taxes that gambling wins entail. But the point is, he still made enough to capitalize Prometheus. That's when we began to dig into the bets he had made and look for any possible organized crime connections.

"Another blind alley. He was absolutely clean. But a funny thing came up while we were checking. Officially, young Rodriguez didn't exist until after his year at Midwestern. Sure, there were references to his academic background that made him acceptable to Midwestern. But they were all filtered through a Board of Education psychiatrist named Myra Sokolow in New York. Part of an equal-opportunity kind of project called UPLIFT. But the trail ended there. Prior records on Rodriguez, stuff that should have been on file, wasn't. The folders had been removed.

The only place we lucked out was on an area check. We discovered Rodriguez's past affiliation with a street gang called the Barons. The group, a minor nuisance in terms of street crime, had become 'hot' politically. Because the break from crime to politics were so sudden and so well organized, we became suspicious of outside influence. We had a file on the Barons here in Maryland. And that's how we got the little we have on Rodriguez.

"At the present time, he is a little over nineteen years of age. He attended New York City public and high schools. All their records on him have disappeared. His attendance at Midwestern is known to both of you, especially you, George. As to what he looks like, reports vary. The man we trailed in New York and couldn't pin down appears to be in his early twenties or late teens. He is six feet tall, about 175 lbs., medium-brown hair, medium complexion, brown, almost hazel eyes. He is well spoken, no trace of any accent except New York regional. Just a moment, George. I see you getting upset. Bear with me.

"Here's the kicker. The description we have for Eduardo Rodriguez tallies exactly with the descriptions we have from abroad on Philippe Martel, Alberto Lugano, and Norberto Cruz! Except for France, the other countries involved don't have the apparatus for checking out a man's background from cradle to grave, as we do. But France says that their man, Martel, doesn't exist on paper before two years ago!

"Naturally, we checked on Rodriguez's comings and goings and put them next to the times when the other men in Prometheus were definitely established as being in Europe. It tallied with times Rodriguez gave our agents the slip here in the States. So as good as Rodriguez is, he still can't be in two places at once. But we can't figure out how he did it! Nobody even vaguely resembling Rodriguez has left the country. Rodriguez doesn't even have a passport!

"And that, gentlemen, is about all we have on Eduardo Rodriguez. The bulk of the files you have before you are comprised of backgrounds on the psychiatrist, Myra Sokolow, his sister, Aida Ruiz, and such contacts as were made at Midwestern. We're completely up a tree, but for one new lead.

"About six months ago, Rodriguez and all his identities abroad began liquidating the resources of Prometheus. Not that it was locked up in much more than money at this point, anyway. Just ten weeks ago, all the other men in Prometheus abroad disappeared as completely as Rodriguez has here. The accounts at each branch of Prometheus contain enough money to pay their staff salaries for the next six months, no more. The money in those accounts is also missing. Taking it all together, it's more than four hundred and fifty million dollars!

"Now here's the newest lead. Six months ago, one of Rodriguez's old street buddies, a Rafael Guzman, bought a building and a business. He did it with winnings from gambling at offtrack betting offices in New York City. He also paid the taxes. Sound familiar?

"So here's what we've got: a man with no past, no reliable description. He has, somewhere, a half billion dollars in four major currencies. He can come and go as he pleases, regardless of the amount of surveillance we place him under. It has been speculated, but not demonstrated to our satisfaction, that he can actually control the will and memory of at least one person, his sister. All other contacts give the same responses his sister did until yesterday. I've sent a flash off to the Chicago office to recheck all the contacts you made at Midwestern, George. We should have the reports back by morning.

"Anything I say past this point is speculation, but, hell, I have to start somewhere. I believe that this Rodriguez kid is the moving force behind it all. I don't think that any government or outside influence such as organized crime is involved. It was one of our first concerns and one we checked out immediately.

"Somehow, someway, he has figured out how to

beat the stock market. Beat it, hell. He can manipulate it. Same as it appears he can manipulate people. He has completely confounded the most sophisticated and best equipped intelligence-gathering organization in the world. He has stolen a huge amount of money and completely disappeared. He . . . excuse me, this may be the call I've been waiting for.

"Yes, this is Henskey. Scramble code ten. Good. You got them out of bed, did you? Yes, I suppose it's justified. I did give you a Ten Priority. They what? Are you sure? . . . I see. That too? . . . All right. Return to Chicago Central. If there are any further orders, I'll call. . . . No! Just stand by, that's all.

"OK, men. That ties it. That was the man I sent out to Midwestern to recheck your interviews, George. Not a one of them can recall ever knowing or hearing of a student named Eduardo Rodriguez. And all his records at the university are gone!

"You men go back to the desk in B wing. I don't want you going back to your hotel. Get accommodations for the next two days. I also want you to draw weapons. Just side arms. I'm putting max security on you guys before both of you develop amnesia, too. I'll see you in the morning. I have to wake up somebody very important right now. And you don't have to hear it. See you both at eight hundred hours back here."

GEORGE T. CASE

What a crock! The second Priority Ten I've ever been a part of, and here I am on ice with Ortiz. I can see Henskey's point of view. Ortiz and I are the only ones who have gotten anything valid on NIETZSCHE. We're also the only ones who haven't been brainwashed into forgetting anything. I guess Henskey figures if either Ortiz or me should bump into NIETZSCHE, knowing what we do, he'd erase us like a couple of spools of tape.

Well, it could be worse. At least I'll be with Henskey as the agents and the computers feed in the information. Maybe I'm getting too old for field work, anyway. Leave it to Ortiz and kids his age. I should be running agents, not running my tail off. But inside work drives me nuts. Just like sitting here. I've read that damn NIETZSCHE file a dozen times, and there's still something there I'm missing. What was it Ortiz said in his report on Aida Ruiz? *If she withheld anything, it would only have been that I didn't know enough to ask her.* But the verbatim report doesn't say any more than his interpretation of what she said. The word-for-word translation just has a lot more "Jesuses" and "God blesses" and "forbids." Must get with Ortiz again at dinner.

He's really very young, though. There's a lot he could have missed. I had to laugh at his expression this morning when he saw ODIN. It is impressive, I must admit. A computer that takes up three quarters of an acre, is tied into every major control system in the country, civilian and military, is quite a gadget.

The spooky part is when it talks to you. That's a new wrinkle since I last visited the ODIN complex. Makes sense, though. Any data you need doesn't have to be encoded by a programmer or even a typist. You just ask the damn thing questions in plain English, and it answers you in the same fashion. That way, any one with the security clearance for ODIN can operate it, and the programmers are separated on a need-to-know basis.

The only people cleared to operate ODIN are Henskey, Charlesworth on the West Coast, the Secretary, and, of course, the President. I'm willing to bet it was the President who Henskey called last night after we left.

But I am surprised at Henskey letting Ortiz into the ODIN complex, and even letting him see and hear the thing at work. Guess if the kid is cleared for a Priority Ten and he sure is, it couldn't do any harm at this point. In for a penny, in for a million. Boy, but that ODIN is fast. It had already drawn a search plan for Rodriguez/NIETZSCHE here and in four other countries. I see now why Hensky gave me such specific orders and interview plans. It wasn't Henskey at all. It was ODIN.

Don't know if I can trust it the way Hensk does, though. A machine, no matter how sophisticated, has no intuition. And it's no smarter than the questions you ask it. It may have the data you need stored away somewhere, but if you don't know how and where to look, it won't volunteer it. I must remember to mention that to young Ortiz. He was looking at the thing like it was a god. Well, maybe to his generation, the computer is a kind of god.

For instance, ODIN has the records and vital statistics on every person living or dead for the past five years in this country. And since it's been taught how to tie in to all the other computers in the system, it's become self-programming to a large extent. It's as though it were alive and growing, learning every day. It knows all, and if you know how to ask it, it tells all. It even can protect itself.

Maybe that's the spookiest part of all. It has an independent power source, protected by God knows how many feet of lead-lined concrete. There are little automatic repair units that go back and forth day after day in little runs too tiny for men except as crawl spaces. The whole thing is interconnected with the little runways, and the service drones scuttle back and forth, checking circuits, repairing when necessary. They even have larger ones that build on to the complex, on orders from ODIN itself. There's still another quarter acre of empty concrete space for it to expand in.

Maybe the thing is alive. After all, it has senses, it grows, regenerates itself, and learns. The only thing it doesn't do is reproduce itself. Although, come to think of it, the remote stations, the ones they use on the west coast to ask it questions, were designed by ODIN, too.

They say the Russians have one like it. I doubt it can touch what we've got. We had a year's head start building ours. And since ODIN became self-programming last year and began gathering data faster than any man or men could, I don't think they'll ever catch up. Thank God for that.

Well, I have time enough to go over the file again before dinner. Damn! I think if I could take a walk outside the compound, in the clean Maryland woods,

I could think better. Inside work gets me down. Whoops! There's the phone. If it's Henskey, there goes dinner!

DARRYL HENSKEY

"Agents Case and Ortiz, meet Professor Martin Grossman. He's with one of our larger university hospitals in the area. His specialty is extrasensory perception. I have told him what he needs to know about our 'hypothetical' missing person. He's come up with a few answers that may be of help. He also has some further questions that only you two can answer. I'm going to remain and . . . excuse me, Professor. This telephone must be answered whenever it rings.

"Yes, this is Henskey. Go ahead. . . . What? . . . What are you people in New York, amateurs? I told you that the pickup had to be . . . it was right, eh? You did get her? Good. Get her down here right away. No! Military transportation. I want that woman completely isolated. No outside contact, understand? You'll be here in less than that or I'll have your head on a plate! Henskey out.

"Good and bad news, men. Professor, you'll have to step outside for a few minutes. I'll ring and have the guard show you out. We'll call you. Thank you.

"Now that he's gone, let's get to this: Aida Ruiz has disappeared. Our people in New York did get Myra Sokolow, though. At Kennedy airport. She was all packed and ready to go. I don't know where. She had no ticket and no reservation in her name on any flight foreign or domestic. Those damn fools in New York panicked and closed in on her at the airport instead of watching her. If they'd only waited, we might have found out how Rodriguez got out of the country without us knowing. If that wasn't bad enough, they didn't even think to pick up Guzman. If one is running, they'll all be running. It may not be too late. I've got the pickup order for him being implemented right now. They're bringing Sokolow down here, too. She should be here by eight. You men get dinner. We may be at this a long time tonight."

RAFAEL GUZMAN

I knew it was too good to last. Man, you no sooner get a little something together, and they come and take it all away. Not that these Feds said anything about it. But I know inside I'm going to lose all I got. The little guy always does. It all came so fast, too.

I'm in the store, and these guys come up and flash their ID cards at me. Not badges, babe. Cards. If they weren't enough, they had the City fuzz with them, too. I don't know what that warrant about taxes is. I know damn well I did exactly what Eddie Rodriguez told me. And when you do exactly like Eddie says, you're OK. The way I figure, they want me for something about Eddie. But I don't think they can hold me without me calling a lawyer.

Like the time they busted the Barons for going after the dudes that was running the tenements uptown. We were right, and our demonstration was legal. Hell, Eddie had us all bailed out inside of two hours after he called the lawyer. If Eddie said that the deal I did to get the store and building was clean, it's clean. Soon as I get a lawyer, I'll be free. But somehow, I don't care too much without Eddie.

When they started in the search of the building, I really was worried. Even though they found the smoke in Pablo's apartment, they didn't seem to care about it. They just left it where it was stashed. They knew what they were looking for, and it wasn't dope. They found those cards that Eddie had sent me from Paris and Rome and Portugal. That's more what they wanted.

When they come to the door to Greenberg's old pad, the one I did like Eddie said with, I really got scared. They didn't ask me for no key either. They just went in, iron door, Fox Lock, and all. Now, I never been inside since I had the place set up with the furniture and groceries. I put the keys under the potatoes downstairs in the store and tried to forget about it, like Eddie said. But I sure wasn't ready for what they found.

The place was full of books I never put inside there. They were stacked so close you could hardly walk around. There was a path from the kitchen table to the john and to the bedroom through the books. Everywhere else was books, four feet high. And I mean books about anything you want to know, and a lot of stuff you couldn't care less about.

There was about half the groceries gone, but no garbage. The dishes was all clean. Outside of all the books, so was the place. Even neater was the way the dude was laid out on the bed. He was wearing the same kind of suit as I was that day, and he

53

looked like he was asleep. But he wasn't. He was dead.

One of the Feds says to me, "Do you know this man?"

"No way," I say.

One of the other Feds says, "What did you expect him to say, Chuck?"

The first Fed says to me, "Have you any idea who he is, or how he got here?"

"I want a lawyer," I say.

"You'll need one," says the other Fed. "That man is Eduardo Rodriguez. You've known him for years. You're coming with us."

"I want a lawyer," I say, but all the time my head is spinning. This dude on the bed is definitely not Eddie Rodriguez, but the Feds think it is. Eddie always told me that if you get busted, never answer any questions. Tell them your name and address. After that, anything they ask, you say, "Ask my lawyer." So that's what I did.

They were taking out that dude from the apartment in a bag at the same time they were hustling me into the back of this unmarked car. I didn't see any ambulance or hospital wagon in front, though. Just a black panel truck.

Now here I am on a plane going somewhere. An army plane, I think. I heard from the pilot talking to the tower on the takeoff that we're going to some place called Anacostia. Wherever that is. I wish I knew where Eddie was. He'd know what to do.

What worries me even more is that dude they found in the bed. I did know him. It was the same guy I saw that day I saw Eddie last. The one who was driving the Mercedes that looked like the one Eddie had. I wish I could reach Eddie.

INTERIM REPORT: PRIORITY TEN (10)

To: District Supervisor Darryl Henskey

From: Office of Forensic Medicine, D.M. Martin, Chief Examiner

Re: PROJECT NIETZSCHE

Sir:

At the request of our New York office, I have performed the postmortem operation on the cadaver supplied by them. The following are the results.

I received for examination the body of a white male, age about twenty. No marks or scars, no indication of any trauma. Subject is six feet, one quarter inch in height. Weight: 175 lbs. Superb physical condition. No defects whatsoever.

Indication of diseases: Negative
Blood chemistry: Normal
Toxology: Negative
    (16 basic poisons, plus 10 best known assasination drugs and toxins):
Vital organs: Negative
    (Disease or toxin traces):
Bone marrow: Negative
    (Disease or toxin traces):
Wounds/punctures: Negative

Radioactivity to MR considered background: Negative

REMARKS:
There is no apparent cause of death. The subject appears to have been in excellent health. There is no evidence whatever to suggest foul play of any sort. Nor can I logically ascribe death to any disease, infectious or degenerative. This subject, by all rules of medicine with which I am familiar, should be alive. But there is no doubt whatsoever that he is dead. As requested, I secured a full set of fingerprints and have forwarded same to your office. Sorry that there is no dental chart. The teeth are in perfect condition; no dental work has ever been performed on this subject.

With your permission, I should like to request the services of Dr. J.G. Yamashita from the Tokyo Bureau. He's the top man in the world in Forensic. Maybe he can find something that I missed.

D.H. Martin

INTERIM REPORT: PRIORITY TEN (10)

To: Secretary of Defense

From: District Supervisor Darryl Henskey, I.G.O. HQ, Greenglade, MD.

Re: PROJECT NIETZSCHE

My dear Mr. Secretary:

Enclosed is a complete summary of Project NIETZSCHE to date. By all logical yardsticks, the case is closed. The body found on the premises of 146 E. 113th St., New York City, has been definitely identified as that of Eduardo Rodriguez. Identification was on the basis of fingerprints taken some years ago. (See subfile: Barons.)

However, the problem of how NIETZSCHE did what he did is no more resolved than it was while he was alive. I am pursuing that aspect through interrogation of Myra Sokolow. (See subfile). Accomplice Guzman has been held incommunicado for over twenty-four hours. Direct violations of his rights. In light of recent investigations into one of our sister agencies, this isn't too healthy a situation.

We have covered by claiming he is in protective custody, and that some person/s unknown are attempting to eradicate all leaders of the Barons. He isn't buying it, but it's the best we've got just now. We have ODIN at work concocting a more credible scenario. Will file further reports as information accumulates.

Have been interrogating Sokolow now for sixteen hours, with breaks. She is unaware that NIETZSCHE is dead. It's my case ace, and I intend to use it this next session.

Regards,

Henskey

TRANSCRIPT: INTERROGATION, MYRA SOKOLOW (6/7)

Session Four (xb: 21. p. 16)

Interrogation was conducted in area B, Greenglade HQ. Monitoring devices all connected directly to ODIN. The ODIN polygraph strips are inserted after each Sokolow response. In addition, there are plain English analyses of the polygraph data. They, also, are by ODIN.

Interrogator was Darryl Henskey, teamed with Field Agt. G.T. Case. Henskey cast as villain, Case as hero. This in light of previous contact with subject by Agt. Case.

CASE: Good afternoon, Dr. Sokolow. So good to see you again.

SOKOLOW: So good to see you, Mr. Case. (*Norm.*)

CASE: I believe you know my superior, Mr. H?

SOKOLOW: We have shared eight of the past sixteen hours, yes. (*Norm.*)

HENSKEY: Listen, Case, let's stop all the nicey-nicey crap and get down to business. This woman is a main figure in a scheme that threatens our national security. This time, you're going to tell us, too, sister.

SOKOLOW: As I have said time and again, I will be delighted to tell you everything I know. Your anger seems to derive from my inability to tell you what I do not know. (*Slt. emot. resp.*)

CASE: I understand, Doctor. But you see, my boss has bosses to answer to, himself.

SOKOLOW: Mr. Case, I am weary. I have been hectored and badgered by this man for the past day and part of the night. I am familiar with the technique you are employing. If I have been adamant with your Mr. "H," it has been for my own reasons. I will no more "open up" to you than I will to him. That is, if I do not choose to do so. At present, I do not choose to do so. (*Pos. resp.*)

HENSKEY: Well, that's all over with now. The whole thing's all over. We're just tying up the loose ends, now. We got your precious Eduardo Rodriguez.

SOKOLOW: Interesting. (*Norm.*)

HENSKEY: Is that all you have to say: "interesting?"

SOKOLOW: What more is there to say? Your saying you have Eduardo doesn't necessarily mean that you do have him. Any more than it makes this a Tax Bureau office, does it, Mr. Case? (*Norm.*)

CASE: It's true, Doctor. We took him twenty-four hours ago.

SOKOLOW: Is the lie coming from you more truthful than from Mr. H? (*Norm.*)

HENSKEY: All right, lady. Do you want to see him? It won't be pretty. You see, he was dead when we found him. And we've done an autopsy. What's left isn't too nice. Would you really want to see what's left?

SOKOLOW: Mr. H., in 1944 I was liberated from an extermination camp in Germany. I am a licensed physician in the state of New York. Do you really think you will shock me? (*Pos. resp.*)

HENSKEY: Have it your way. Here are the pictures. Here's a partial autopsy report. What do you say now?

SOKOLOW: I say that I have seen some pictures. Show me the body. (*Pos. resp.*)

CASE: If we can arrange for you to view the body, will you tell us what we need to know?

SOKOLOW: I make no promises. If I am satisfied that the body you have is genuinely Eddie Rodriguez, I will tell you all I know. I would also like to be disconnected from your polygraph. (*Pos resp.*)

HENSKEY: What are you talking about?

SOKOLOW: Oh, come now, Mr. H. I've seen designs for chairs like this. Where is the operator? The next room perhaps? (*Pos. resp.*)

CASE: No use trying to fool you, is there? Yes, the operator is on the floor below you. The chair leads go through the base and into the floor.

SOKOLOW: Then, let us go view this body you claim is Eddie. (*Norm.*)

HENSKEY: Not claim, lady, *is*.

SOKOLOW: As you wish. (*Alert input disc.*)

TRANSCRIPT: INTERROGATION, MYRA SOKOLOW (6/7)

Session Four B (xb: b21. p. 14)

Personnel are identical to Session Four.

HENSKEY: Are you satisfied, now that you've seen him?

SOKOLOW: I am satisfied, yes. Incidentally, you may either disconnect your polygraph, or I shall sit in another chair. (*Pos. resp.*)

CASE: How about this one, Doctor?

SOKOLOW: I'm not that naïve, Mr. Case. I shall sit in Mr. H.'s chair. (*Alert input disc.*)

CASE: There. Are you more comfortable now, Doctor?

SOKOLOW: Yes, thank you. (*Contact resumes. Pos. resp.*)

CASE: Now, suppose you tell us about Eddie Rodriguez.

SOKOLOW: To do that, I shall have to tell you a history of events that have not yet occurred. A future history, if you prefer. (*Pos. resp.*)

HENSKEY: Look, I don't understand this.

SOKOLOW: Nor shall you ever, unless you let me tell this my own way, at my own pace. (*Pos. resp.*)

CASE: We're sorry. Please continue, Dr. Sokolow.

SOKOLOW: Very well. But this will take some time. I am tired and hungry. I do not sleep well in confinement. A souvenir of my childhood. In addition, there will be a number of points in my narrative

61

you will either question or outright disbelieve. I think you will want to have present a theoretical mathematician, a competent neurologist with a specialty in extrasensory perception, and a polygraph operator actually in the room. You see, there are responses that a polygraph operator can clarify more easily if the subject is visible. (*Pos. resp.*)

HENSKEY: What's wrong with right now? I've got all the time in the world, lady. I can have all the people you need here in . . . twenty-five minutes.

SOKOLOW: I do not choose to tell you right now. I wish to sleep in a comfortable bed. I want a good breakfast. Then I shall tell you. (*Pos. resp.*)

CASE: Will you excuse us a moment, Doctor?

SOKOLOW: Of course. I don't really care what you say or think, anyway. You could just as easily speak in front of me rather than in that corner, there. You do look a bit foolish. (*Pos. resp.*)

HENSKEY: What do you think, George?

CASE: I think she's dead right, Hensk. We do look silly huddled over here talking. Especially when the whole room is on the air, so to speak.

HENSKEY: That's not what I mean, and you know it. Do you think she's telling the truth? Or is she stalling for time?

CASE: If she were lying at any point, you would have got the flash from ODIN, wouldn't you?

HENSKEY: True. All right, I'll go along. But something doesn't smell right to me.

CASE: Nothing about this project has to me since I first got your orders.

HENSKEY: Very well, Dr. Sokolow. I'll ring for the matron. You'll get all you want. But I warn you, I will get what I want as well.

SOKOLOW: You will get what you asked for. As to

whether it is what you want or not, I couldn't say. Ah, that light would mean my guard has arrived, yes? (*Norm.*)

CASE: Come in, Matron. Will you please escort Dr. Sokolow to her quarters?

(*Alert input disc.*)

SOKOLOW: You are too kind, Mr. Case. And good-night, Mr. Henskey.

HENSKEY: What did you say?

SOKOLOW: I said good-night.

HENSKEY: Not that. What did you call me?

SOKOLOW: Mr. Henskey. It *is* Henskey, isn't it?

HENSKEY: Now just a damn minute . . .

SOKOLOW: Now, now. We agreed about tomorrow, didn't we? Until then . . .

HENSKEY: That will be all, Matron. Return Dr. Sokolow to this room at ten hundred hours tomorrow.

MATRON: Yes sir.

(*Door Close*)

CASE: Well, what the hell do you make of that?

HENSKEY: I make it that my senior field agent got careless. You weren't watching. You dropped my name to her somewhere. If you weren't sitting down, I'd kick your ass.

CASE: You're dead wrong, Hensk. I never dropped your name. If you doubt me, ask ODIN. (*Pos. resp.*)

HENSKEY: I'll be damned! (*Insuf. Data*)

INTERIM REPORT: PRIORITY TEN (10)

To: Secretary of Defense

From: District Supervisor, Darryl Henskey, I.G.O.
HQ, Greenglade, MD.

Re: PROJECT NIETZSCHE

Dear Mr. Secretary:

Enclosed is the transcript of the Sokolow interview. In view of the events of the past few weeks,
it's as good an explanation as any I've been able to
come up with.

I must add, in all fairness, that I did not believe
it when I heard it. But I can't disbelieve what happened. I have not edited the tapes, nor removed any
part, no matter how small, from the transcript.

I will, in view of what befell him, recommend
Agent Ortiz for the highest decoration possible. I
don't know how much consolation that will be to
his parents. I feel like I'm back in Korea writing
letters to next of kin again.

Sincerely,

Henskey

TRANSCRIPT: INTERROGATION, MYRA SOKOLOW (6/8)

Session Five (xb: 22. p. 18)

Interrogation conducted in Area C, Greenglade HQ. Monitoring devices all connected directly to ODIN. Polygraph strips and an analyses of same under separate cover. All responses by Sokolow recorded as truth. Analyses of interrogation team polygraphs, except where subterfuge was deliberately used in questioning, are equally verifiable as within polygraph limits of true statements.

Interrogation team composed of Darryl Henskey, Field Age. G. T. Case, plus two experts in fields requested by Sokolow in previous interview. (See: xb: b21.)

EXPERT TEAM:

Martin Grossman, M.D., psychiatrist, neurologist, head of Special Committee for Investigation into Extrasensory Phenomena at Capitol University. (Full biography in personnel folder, separate cover.) Security clearance upgraded from Priority Seven to Ten (10) by special order, D.F. Henskey, on 6/7.

Leonard A. Klein, Ph.D., Chairman, Mathematics Dept., Capitol University. Code designation: DIOGENES. (Dr. Klein is one of our agents. See personnel folder.) Klein already cleared for security up to level Ten (10).

HENSKEY: Good morning, gentlemen. I would like you to meet Field Agent Case. The lady seated between us is Dr. Myra Sokolow from New York City. Dr. Sokolow is a medical doctor and a psychoanalyst. You both are here at her request. I realize that it's unusual not to have files to which you may refer. However, the security aspect of this case forbids duplication of the master file. You have been given foolscap pads and pens for your own notes. At the time this interview concludes, you will turn over these materials to the Marine Corps guard at the door to this room. They will, of course, be destroyed. All information on this case is to be regarded as a Priority Ten matter. I see Dr. Grossman has a question.

GROSSMAN: I do. Just what is a Priority Ten?

HENSKEY: Sorry. I forgot that your ties to I.G.O. are intellectual only. Priority Ten is the highest form of security we have classified. It is used only when a grave threat to national security is possible by silence being breached.

GROSSMAN: I see. Does having this knowledge place any of us in jeopardy physically, or will we have to be sequestered once we are privy to the information?

HENSKEY: I really wish I could answer that, Doctor. If the Agency feels that you might be in danger, you will be given the necessary protection. Your best protection, actually, is silence. In addition, you will be given only such information as is necessary to form an opinion of this case.

GROSSMAN: I then assume we are here to hear a hypothetical case.

HENSKEY: I wish it were, Doctor. You will be listening to a hypothetical explanation for a very real case. In some instances, Agent Case and myself will ask questions that you will not understand. They deal with specifics of this case and as such will be meaningless to you. Please consider these queries on a need-to-know basis. Understood?

GROSSMAN: Understood.

HENSKEY: Dr. Sokolow?

SOKOLOW: Thank you. First, good morning, Martin.

GROSSMAN: How are you, Myra? It's been too long. When was it, the Philadelphia convention three years ago?

SOKOLOW: Ah, Martin. Still playing parlor games. I'm sure the organization which has brought us here knows that you have an eidetic memory and could tell us all exactly when and where we last met, down to about ninety percent accuracy. Mr. Henskey, are you aware that Dr. Grossman and I were colleagues at Bellevue Hospital in New York City from 1964 to 1968?

HENSKEY: No, madam, I was not. Are you, or were you, personally involved?

SOKOLOW: I am involved personally with all mankind, Mr. Henskey. Are you asking me if Dr. Grossman and I were or are still lovers?

HENSKEY: Yes.

SOKOLOW: The answer is yes, we were and no, we are not. We have not seen each other nor have we spoken or corresponded in the past three years. In any event, our relationship had nothing to do with the present case. I wasn't all that involved at the time. But where is your polygraph operator? You can verify that easily enough.

HENSKEY: Let us assume that you are visible to your polygraph operator. Please proceed, Dr. Sokolow.

SOKOLOW: Interesting. You, sir, I do not know.

KLEIN: I am Leonard Klein. I am Chairman of Mathematics at a university nearby.

SOKOLOW: Excellent. To begin with, I should like to relate this history to you in a straight narrative form. If you and Dr. Grossman can hold your questions until I finish, I believe we can save a great deal of back and forth. I don't ask anyone here to pass on whether what I am about to say is true or not. I only wish your opinion as to whether it *could* be true. Further, your opinions are for the benefit of the two men seated with me at this table. For myself, I believe everything that I will tell you is unassailably accurate.

KLEIN: Very well. If we can get on with this. I have commitments at the university.

SOKOLOW: I understand. First, let us speak of the far, far future. Let us assume that the species of man will survive the usual number of wars, plagues, and natural disasters, as it has in the past. The difference is that man will become, in the absence of all his vanquished natural enemies, a threat to his own continued survival.

The planet Earth will be almost depleted of its ability to support life. Man himself will have changed. Not just in the physical ways that have been speculated upon by evolutionists and radiologists. Happily, he will have matured intellectually and emotionally.

Our present great god, technology, will have fallen. Oh, a number of artifacts will remain, but man will have returned, after countless years, to his beginnings. He will live simply and peacefully amid the remains of his destroyed ecology.

KLEIN: Dr. Sokolow. In deference to what I'm sure are excellent credentials on your part, I did not come

68

here to listen to some fairy tale about some speculative future time.

SOKOLOW: I believe I've already pointed out that what is at issue here is not certainty, but probability. Furthermore, we have not yet come to that part of my 'fairy tale', as you put it, which involves your expertise. May I please continue?

KLEIN: Very well.

SOKOLOW: Thank you. As I was saying, this future man of which I speak lives in a series of oases on a near-desolated Earth, where he conserves what little remains of its resources. The attempt to find compatible life forms, or even near-life within our solar system, has failed. Insofar as our particular sun and planets are concerned, we are alone.

Expeditions to other star systems are never heard from again and after Earth's last, nearly totally destructive war, there are no longer the resources, nor is there the desire, to try once more to reach other planets. It is at this point that man, at last, turns inward. He begins to explore his inner potential. A useful form of telepathy is developed, and with this, all further hostilities cease. You see, telepaths cannot lie to each other. And wars, after all, are founded on deception and secrecy. Or should I say "security," Mr. Henskey?

HENSKEY: Do you really want an answer to that question, Doctor?

SOKOLOW: No, I suppose not. But back to my fairy tale. With telepathy, great breakthroughs are made in the field of what Dr. Grossman, in a recent paper, has termed "Inner Space." These are the latent powers that all men possess to communicate, move themselves, and objects as well—to foresee future events with no more equipment than their minds.

Ironically, it is through the powers he has all along, that man finds a way to escape his impoverished planet. Through centuries of concentrated effort, man is at last able to isolate the thing we call intellect, or if we are religious, the soul, from its physical envelope, the body. Suddenly, all the laws of physics and mathematics which govern man's movements no longer pertain.

The nature of this . . . soul, if you will, is pure energy. But it is not energy in the sense we have known. It is not any form of electromagnetic energy; a wave form. It is not bound by physical laws which govern such forms. It is the real force that activates all energy. It is the force of creation itself.

Odd, isn't it? All the years that man searched for the secrets of the universe and god, both were to be found within himself. But man didn't even start to look for these things within himself until he was faced with extinction. A great pity, but again, typical of man.

HENSKEY: *Doctor,* I realize that you must tell this in your own way, but I am responsible to some very present tense authorities both inside and outside my agency. Will you soon come to something that bears on our case?

SOKOLOW: Yes, I shall. Right now. When I spoke of leaving a planet which could no longer sustain physical life, I may have misled you. Through a group effort, the population of our future earth was able to shed the hulls which bound it to the planet. No personalities survived. All individuals melded themselves into one mass of living energy, embodying a group consciousness. A *gestalt,* if you will. Then, no longer bound by physical laws, that living energy was capable of going on forever. Call it man's ultimate evolution; call it what you like. It exists. Or it will, some time from now.

There was only one problem: Of the five-hundred-thousand-odd remaining beings on future Earth, about two percent were unable to complete the separation process. They were what we would call wards of the society: genetically flawed, throwbacks, sports. We make up new names for them ourselves every few years. Once they were called idiots, or morons. Then retarded, or brain-damaged. Most recently they are termed "special persons," which indeed, they are.

In the future, these unfortunates are cared for by the society. But when the time for man to change his life form comes, they are only capable of half the process. Although they can, with their limited powers, separate themselves from their body shells, their personalities are such that they cannot be absorbed into the new *gestalt* that will be man. A solution is devised: Before man, as we know him, departs the planet, he has to find a safe place for those who cannot follow. That place is the physical past of the planet Earth.

KLEIN: Preposterous! You are talking about traveling in time. It can't be done. It's a common speculation based on a misconception. Time isn't linear; it's not a road you can travel up and down, nor an elevator you can ride and get off at various levels. Time is physical, as well as duration. A year ago, Earth was physically in a different place in space. It remained there for a microsecond, because the planet is in constant motion, as is the entire galaxy, then moved on. You can't go back. Even if you could, what would you use for a reference point? It's the same as saying that you can always find that good fishing spot in the ocean, because when you first found it, you made a mark on the side of the boat!

Mr. Henskey, I have been associated with some odd-ball projects through this agency in the past, but this one takes the prize. I'm surprised that you let it get this far . . .

HENSKEY: Are you saying, then, Dr. Klein, that none of this can be remotely possible?

KLEIN: Absolutely not!

HENSKEY: Even if, as Dr. Sokolow says, none of the existing laws of mathematics and physics cover the situation?

KLEIN: Now, just a moment here. If you want to say that something can be so, exclusive of the facts and all laws of science, that's different. If you accept the premise, then anything can be so. On that basis, I can say that the future Earth of which Dr. Sokolow speaks will one day turn into a stale bagel. Who is to say I'm wrong?

HENSKEY: Then it could be so?

KLEIN: On those terms, anything could be so. I consider the likelihood as valid as the stale bagel idea I just gave you. I think you'd have to attend a few years of classes in my field to even understand my reasons.

HENSKEY: I'm sure. But time is important here.

KLEIN: Don't you see? Time is exactly what we're talking about. Let this woman believe what she believes. I have no doubt that she's sincere about this pipe dream. But if she believes it, it doesn't mean I have to. I can't take it on faith. I'm sorry. Faith isn't enough!

SOKOLOW: I must differ with you. In this case, faith is everything. It is only by complete acceptance of the powers that exist within us that we can use them at all.

KLEIN: We're getting nowhere. Will there be any further need for my technical advice? I can't take much more of this crap.

HENSKEY: Frankly, I don't know. It's Dr. Sokolow's ball game. Doctor, how about it?

SOKOLOW: I don't think we can go much further if Dr. Klein's mind is closed on the subject.

KLEIN: Madam, my mind is closed on the subject of folderol that any undergraduate in physics could refute!

HENSKEY: In that case, Dr. Klein, you are free to go. You will observe complete Priority Ten on what you have heard.

KLEIN: Don't worry about it. Even if I did tell anyone, I'd be laughed right out of my tenure at the university. No, I promise you that I'll try to forget this morning completely by this afternoon. It won't take much effort, either.

HENSKEY: I'll ring for the guard. (Buzz)

GUARD: Yes, sir?

HENSKEY: Please see Dr. Klein here through Area A and call for his car.

GUARD: Very good, sir.

HENSKEY: Good morning, Dr. Klein.

KLEIN: For you, perhaps.

GROSSMAN: Now that Dr. Klein has left, can we continue with our hypothetical, true case history? I'm frankly dubious, but I know Myra, er, Dr. Sokolow's capabilities so well, I feel we should hear her out.

SOKOLOW: Thank you, Martin. I think we can go more quickly, now. I hadn't expected too different a reaction from Dr. Klein. I was warned, but I knew that Mr. Henskey would have wanted someone like Dr. Klein present.

CASE: Warned by whom?

SOKOLOW: By the man whose body your coroner dissected last night.

HENSKEY: Then can we please get on with this? We still haven't come to anything which bears on this case.

SOKOLOW: Ah, but we have! You see, when these "special people" were sent to the past of Earth, they did not just float about in the form of pure energy, although some did and still do. We call them ghosts, spirits, poltergeists.

No, we are concerned with those who did something else. Some of them have entered into the bodies and minds of living men and women at various stages of our planet's history. Depending upon their degree of success in entering the host body and mind, we have a whole dictionary of terms: demonic possession, insanity, *idiot savant,* genius, monster and, yes . . . Messiah!

GROSSMAN: Myra! Do you mean to tell me that . . .

SOKOLOW: Please, Martin. If you have ever trusted me, please let me finish! Let us say that the initial contact can only be made when the host's body and mind are at the threshold of death. Past that point, only a momentary disorientation or a physical trauma are necessary for transfer to still another host body.

CASE: This is getting a little heavy for me.

SOKOLOW: It would be for anyone. I am asking you to put aside virtually everything you've ever accepted as true. But in your acceptance, haven't there always been questions, questions that the rules don't cover?

CASE: What kind of questions?

SOKOLOW: This sort. Martin, what causes a genius? Please answer directly, and in terms that Mr. Case won't find "heavy."

GROSSMAN: We don't know. Is that a direct enough answer?

SOKOLOW: What is the nature of extrasensory perception, telepathy, psychokinesis, clairvoyance?

GROSSMAN: We don't know. That's why we're studying it.

CASE: Hell, I don't even know what psychokin-whatchimacallit is.

GROSSMAN: It's the ability to affect the movement of bodies in motion, or to actually start and stop them by using the powers of the mind. The most common example of this thing is the gambler's "lucky" streak at dice or roulette.

CASE: Are you saying there's no such thing as luck?

GROSSMAN: On the contrary. There are laws of averages. Dr. Klein, if he hadn't stormed off, would be able to tell you a lot more about them than I. What I am saying is that we have documented evidence that certain people can alter the laws of probability and motion by concentrating on doing it. I published a book on the subject just last year. It's called *Exploring Inner Space*.

CASE: I'm afraid I'm not much of a reader.

GROSSMAN: I'm afraid you're not alone. The book was disputed hotly in many circles. I was hoping that my colleagues would be more receptive than they were. Their reaction was not too different from Dr. Klein's.

CASE: Gee, I'm sorry, Dr. Grossman.

GROSSMAN: Me too. But Myra, are you saying that all ESP is attributable to these "psychic possessions?"

SOKOLOW: Not at all. Everyone possesses these powers to a certain extent. It is only when a host with the potential is inhabited that the effects I will describe to you take place.

GROSSMAN: There are physical indications, then?

SOKOLOW: Under ideal circumstances, yes. If the host is talented in terms of being able to develop extra or paranormal senses, the "visitor," let's call it, has the same reaction you would to finding the ideal house in which to live. But there is no ideal house. There are always little things one wants: an extra room here, improved wiring there, perhaps a whole new plumbing system. One of the prime signs of a "visitor" having found a proper host is the way that he begins to redecorate, as it were. Faulty heart valves become whole. Scar tissue becomes healthy. Bone breaks which have been improperly set straighten out. Lost teeth grow in again . . .

CASE: What about dental work? Fillings, crowns . . . root canals?

SOKOLOW: I know your motive for that question, Mr. Case. Yes, if teeth have been filled, new tooth tissue, growing from beneath them, will push out the old fillings. Just such a thing happened in Eddie's case.

GROSSMAN: Eddie?

HENSKEY: A moment, please, Dr. Sokolow. We're getting into an area where the information given Dr. Grossman can be a threat. Both to him and us.

SOKOLOW: I told you that I would give all the facts as I know them. I wasn't aware that I would have to precensor all that I said in terms of your security problems. I can't do that. I don't even know what your rules are. I would suggest that if you trust Dr. Grossman enough to have him here, you could trust him enough to tell him the entire story. From this point on, I shall have to be quite specific, as I don't have direct knowledge of any other cases of "visitation." Do you want to have another of your quaint conferences with Mr. Case?

76

HENSKEY: We are concerned with the physical safety of Dr. Grossman as well as our security. If we make him privy to all that's happened, we can't let him return to his job at the university until we're satisfied the threat to national security is ended. And we don't have the legal power to keep him from his job.

GROSSMAN: Keep me from my job? This is my job! And if what Myra says is so, you couldn't keep me away from here! I consult with the I.G.O. only because you have managed to get funding for my research. I work here to pay it back. But this, this is my real work, right here. Hell, if I had a bag packed, I'd start in now!

HENSKEY: I'm afraid it's not that easy. We must devise a cover story for your leaving the university; somehow estimate how long you'll be gone. Most important, I have to make a phone call to get approval. It may take a few hours.

GROSSMAN: Fine with me. I'm ready for some lunch, if we can't go on right now.

HENSKEY: Good idea. I'll ring for the guard. *(Buzz)* Enjoy your lunch.

GUARD: Yes, sir?

HENSKEY: Please bring these people to the Area A commissary. You will remain with them and escort them back here at . . . er, fourteen hundred hours. They are not to be out of your sight, do you understand?

GUARD: Yes, sir. But what about the lady?

HENSKEY: Of course, her too.

GUARD: Oh, yes, I understood that part. But I can't watch the lady all the time. . . . I mean, there's . . . uh . . .

SOKOLOW: I think your guard is wondering if he is to hold my hand in the ladies' room.

77

HENSKEY: Oh, Christ. I forgot. All right. Have the O.O.D. detail a WAC guard to her. In the meantime, get them out of here. I have some calls to make. No, no, Case, dammit. I want you here for now.

(Door close)

HENSKEY: Well, George. What do you think?

CASE: I don't know. I can't bring myself to believe it. What does the ODIN polygraph say about her?

HENSKEY: It says she's been telling the truth, or what she believes to be the truth, straight down the line. I think I'm going to take the chance and let Grossman in on it.

CASE: Aren't you going to call whoever it is you call?

HENSKEY: Come on, George. You're a grown man. You'll have this job someday, God help you. I'd have to call the Secretary and the President both. And you know it. I will, of course, but only to say that we need Grossman's expertise. If I told either the Secretary or the President why, we'd both be in a rubber room before Sokolow and Grossman were back from lunch.

CASE: Do you think you're doing the right thing, keeping the big boys in the dark?

HENSKEY: It's only until after lunch. They'll get the transcript tomorrow anyway. Besides, NIETZSCHE is dead. We just have to find out how he did what he did. And we seem to be getting there. It would take too long to brief the Secretary and the President.

CASE: OK, Hensk. You're the guy that plays with the big boys.

HENSKEY: I don't know as you show the proper respect for our superiors, George. They have titles, you know.

CASE: What the hell are you talking about? This is you and me, Hensk.

HENSKEY: Yeah. Just you and me and the transcript of all we've said, which they both will have copies by tomorrow.

CASE: Jesus! Is that thing still on?

HENSKEY: It's never off, George.

CASE: Oh, wow.

HENSKEY: Enjoy your lunch, George. I have some calls to make.

(END TRANSCRIPT)

GEORGE CASE

Sometimes I think Henskey does it on purpose to keep me off balance. Like keeping the transcript running after the interrogation was over. Unless the damn thing *does* run automatically while there's someone in the room. I'm lucky I didn't refer to the big boys the way I usually do. I'd be out inspecting fruit at the California border next week.

Saw Ortiz at lunch. Gee, that's a good kid. While he's been cooped up here, he's been doing all kinds of paper work. He wants to take the Grad 5 exam in the fall. When I told him that working on a Priority Ten automatically advanced him one grade, he lit up like a neon sign. When he went right back to the exam. prep. booklet he was reading, I asked him why bother? Know what he said? "Well, Mr. Case. If I'm a Grade 5 now, I should know this stuff anyway. Besides, the Grade 6 exam will be based in part on the stuff I have to know for Grade 5."

Can you beat it? He's upper grade material for sure. Except I don't know how good he'd be in an improv. situation. That sort of flexibility only comes with experience. As an inside man on the Latin American section, he'd be invaluable. But sometimes you get a feeling about an outside man. There are innies and outies. I've been an outie all my life.

But I wonder if Henskey was serious about me taking over the district when he's ready to leave? I don't know if I'd even want the job. Like today, for instance. I don't think I would have taken the chance on letting Grossman in on NIETZSCHE. Especially in view of his past relationship with Sokolow. Then, again, if he had tried to brief the big boys over the phone, I don't think they'd have believed him. Hell, I was there, and I still don't buy this whole story Sokolow's been spinning.

The loose ends on this case are too many and too complicated. I still get the feeling that there's something I'm missing. Right under my nose. Like the time in Germany when our own section head went over to the other side. I'd been delivering Priority Seven and Eight stuff to him for months and not feeling right about it. I've got the same feeling now. Not that I distrust Henskey. Hell, he's married to the Agency. For real, now, since his wife died. I'm willing to bet that he hasn't been outside the Greenglade complex in a month.

Well, back to the NIETZSCHE windup. Told Ortiz that if he wanted to monitor the proceedings, he could follow it all on the ODIN repeater in the basement. Gave him clearance with Internal Security. He'd need it. No one below Grade 8 is allowed in there alone. Technically, Henskey or I should be with him. But if Hensk cleared him for a Priority Ten, I can take the authority to pass him in alone. After all, NIETZSCHE is dead. I must remember to tell Henskey that he's down there, though.

Transcript: Interrogation,
Myra Sokolow (6-8)

Session Five B (xb: b23. p. 12)

Continuation of previous session Area C Greenglade
HQ. Monitoring devices as previous. Team as before,
minus DIOGENES, who left in mid-session of (xb: 22).

HENSKEY: Welcome back, Doctors. I've made the
necessary calls. Dr. Grossman is cleared for all
aspects of NIETZSCHE.

SOKOLOW: I take it that NIETZSCHE is the name
you've given to Eddie. It fits, in a limited way. It's
also gratifying to know that someone in this agency
reads.

GROSSMAN: Now, Myra. I'm part of this agency
myself. A consultant, it's true, but still a part. You
must get over the idea that the I.G.O. is some kind of
monster. It serves a purpose. The other side has an
outfit that makes the I.G.O. look like the Campfire
Girls. What we've done here is only for self-defense.

HENSKEY: Well said, Dr. Grossman. Shall we proceed?

GROSSMAN: By all means.

SOKOLOW: Do you wish me to continue talking in
circles, still?

HENSKEY: No, that won't be necessary. But to
avoid covering the same ground, I've brought the
NIETZSCHE file for Dr. Grossman to go over. That's
the red-bordered file at your chair, Doctor. Why
don't you look through it while I ask Dr. Sokolow a
few questions unrelated to what we've been discussing?

GROSSMAN: Very well. Give me about five minutes.

CASE: Are you sure that's enough time for the file, Dr. Grossman?

SOKOLOW: More than enough. Martin reads and retains at a startling rate. What was it you wished to ask me, Mr. Henskey?

HENSKEY: It has to do with our session yesterday. You knew my name. How?

SOKOLOW: I'm afraid that your question does bear on what we've been discussing, after all. I was given your name and description by Eddie. He telephoned and told me to go to Kennedy Airport with a packed bag. He said that I would be picked up by someone and brought to you at this place.

HENSKEY: He what?

SOKOLOW: Yes, Mr. Henskey. Eddie knows who and what you are. I would guess that all that's happened in the past few days has been part of a plan he had.

HENSKEY: Then there's been a leak.

SOKOLOW: Not necessarily. You can't keep secrets from a telepath.

CASE: You can if he's never met you. No one except lower grade operatives has ever had any contact with NIETZSCHE. None of them knows Mr. Henskey's name or job.

SOKOLOW: But you do, Mr. Case.

CASE: But I've never even seen NIETZSCHE.

SOKOLOW: Ah, but you have. And he, you. Do you remember the day at my office, the patient that came in just as you left?

CASE: Of course. A young woman, blond, about twenty-two. Thin, five-four, no marks visible. Wore a print blouse, white skirt with pleats. White shoes, handbag with large brass clasp.

SOKOLOW: Excellent! Except for one small detail.

CASE: Which is?

SOKOLOW: The person you saw was Eddie Rodriguez. Forgive me for not referring to him as NIETZSCHE. The name has unpleasant connotations for me.

CASE: In drag? There's nothing in the file to indicate that he ever so much as went near the gays. I even . . .

GROSSMAN: I'm finished with the file, Mr. Henskey.

HENSKEY: Already? Good.

CASE: Just a minute. I want to stay with this line of questioning. If I was had by a subject in drag, it was the best piece of work I've ever run into.

SOKOLOW: I told you earlier that it bears on what I was telling you. The explanation lies in what Eddie has become.

HENSKEY: *Has* become?

SOKOLOW: Please. May I tell this in my own way? Your questions should answer themselves as we go along.

HENSKEY: Very well.

SOKOLOW: As I was saying before lunch, when Eddie was taken to Lenox Hill Hospital with meningitis, he was in the right state to be inhabited by one of our "visitors." As Mr. Case has already guessed, the "visitor" took up residence in Eddie at that time.

GROSSMAN: I assumed as much from reading the file. That's why you asked about fillings, wasn't it, Mr. Case?

CASE: Exactly.

GROSSMAN: This is fascinating, Myra. What other physical changes were effected? I mean, I see by the file about his growth while at school. It's all within the realm of possibility of natural growth. Such things do occur in adolescence.

SOKOLOW: If we stick to the chronological order of events, I think you'll find that answer as well.

GROSSMAN: Yes, of course. I'm sorry, Myra. Please continue.

SOKOLOW: Well, on entering Eddie's body, the "visitor" began to make immediate changes. The first was to cure the meningitis. The second was to expand Eddie's telepathic sense. When he spoke "in tongues," as his sister so quaintly puts it, he was only picking up the thought patterns of a Pakistani nurse nearby. She evidently has strong latent telepathic abilities. Many eastern people do. I believe it has to do with the training of the mind that their religions give to them.

Further, when Eddie spoke the rest of the verse from the psalms, he was only getting the words from his sister's mind as she read from the Bible.

GROSSMAN: Then it was Eddie speaking, not the "visitor?"

SOKOLOW: I can only speculate. As Eddie has explained it to me, once the change was effected, there was no difference between him and the "visitor." They immediately shared all that Eddie knew, as well as all the new stimuli that he encountered, such as the Pakistani nurse's thoughts and language. The meningitis-induced coma left him almost the instant the "visitor" took up residence.

GROSSMAN: What did this knowledge do to Eddie, himself?

SOKOLOW: He was completely unaware of the "visitor." It was as though he had begun to function better, no more. The awareness of the "visitor" came much later. One would suppose that immediate knowledge would have driven him mad. It has others.

HENSKEY: My God! You mean that there are more like him?

SOKOLOW: No, not quite like Eddie. Mr. Henskey, I'm sure you know that there are forms of mental illness that completely baffle science. I have recently discovered, through Eddie, the explanation. These afflicted poor are the results of improper or sometimes clumsy joining with "visitors."

GROSSMAN: How can a creature so advanced make such mistakes?

SOKOLOW: First off, Martin, they are not "creatures." They are human beings, not too different from you and me. They are our descendants. Some are clever, some are not. Some are beneficent; others, willful. Further, they are the handicapped of their generation, mentally.

HENSKEY: Then this thing that was inside NIETZSCHE was insane?

SOKOLOW: The term insane has no meaning. If you mean they did not come within the boundaries their society considered the norm, yes. By today's standards and your terminology, they would be called retarded or idiots. But in our society, they would be supermen. And as all individuals, their intelligence and abilities to use it vary greatly. In Eddie's case, we have the combination of great latent powers in the host, plus a rather bright "visitor." The result is what has us all here.

HENSKEY: Then there are more like him!

SOKOLOW: Tens of thousands. There always have been. Read your history with new eyes. The list is impressive. The degree of their success is also an indication of the natural talents of the host and the abilities of the "visitor" in each case.

GROSSMAN: Leonardo?

SOKOLOW: Yes.

GROSSMAN: Einstein?

SOKOLOW: Yes. As well as Genghis Kahn, his grandson, Kublai Kahn, Attila, Alexander, Caesar, Napoleon, Hitler . . .

HENSKEY: This is worse than I though! You mean we could have been dealing with another Hitler?

SOKOLOW: Or another Buddha, Moses, Ghandi, or Christ. As I say, the way the relationship between host and "visitor" develops is based on the abilities and leanings of both.

GROSSMAN: What about Freud?

SOKOLOW: One of the first questions I asked, Martin. No, he was a very talented man, but only a man using his own, unenhanced abilities. Oddly, knowing this made me respect him more.

HENSKEY: And what is NIETZSCHE? Devil, saint, philosopher?

SOKOLOW: All of these things, at one time or another. You must understand. The "visitor" could not inform Eddie of its presence until the "remodeling" of the host was completed. Eddie had to be brought to a point in education where his mind was able to grasp what had happened without going into catatonic shock. For the better part of a year, Eddie was a street kid from Spanish Harlem with the abilities of a Napoleon or an Attila.

CASE: I can believe that. I've seen the record on the Barons.

SOKOLOW: Another interesting aspect of the case. It's where I came into it. I thought that after my preliminary sessions with Eddie, that I'd come upon an undiscovered genius of fantastic potential. A rose growing on a dung heap. I tried to instill some of the more conventional morality in him. Don't forget, he was a slum child with a slum dweller's values. Survival was first. It amazed me how quickly he absorbed all I had to offer. There were sessions when after he'd gone, I felt like a wrung-out sponge. Within weeks, he reorganized the Barons into a positive force in the community. I was convinced at this point that all he needed was an education to be one of the great men of all time. I arranged for the scholarship at Midwestern. But Eddie was the one who insisted it be an athletic scholarship. He prepared himself for it in the space of six weeks.

GROSSMAN: And none of this aroused any suspicions in your mind that this was a case for continued study, perhaps for consultation and publication?

SOKOLOW: Naturally it did. I broached the subject to him early on. He refused to cooperate. There was no way I could make him demonstrate his amazing abilities if he did not choose to. Had I published his accomplishments without being able to substantiate them, I would have been a laughingstock.

CASE: He pulled the same stunt on his professors at Midwestern.

SOKOLOW: I know he did. And the most incredible aspect of it all was the way he grew in abilities by the day. It wasn't a rising curve. It was a series of quantum jumps. I remember the day he became fully telepathic.

HENSKEY: What do you mean, fully?

SOKOLOW: Up until that time, he had been extraordinarily sensitive to the moods and emotions of others. We, in our analyst/patient relationship, established working rapport in the first twenty minutes of the first session.

HENSKEY: The significance of that misses me, Doctor.

GROSSMAN: If I may, Mr. Henskey. It's roughly the equivalent of a math student grasping calculus, after twenty minutes of training in geometry.

SOKOLOW: I wouldn't know. But I do know that

after seven weeks of daily sessions, he could gain no more from any further time with me. I recall the day quite clearly. We were working on the feelings he had experienced at the loss of his parents. It happened at a particularly sensitive age, as you all know from his file. I was attempting to explain to him that such a loss is by no means unusual; that others have experienced similar tragedies and worked them out. He looked at me and said, "You mean, like the day you saw your mother and father shot? She was wearing the blue dress with the white collar. It was a bright fall day . . ." Half in wonder, half in horror, I listened as he recounted to me every detail of the day. When he finished, he put his hand on mine and said, "I understand." For the first time in my life, someone said those words to me, and I knew them to be absolutely, undeniably true. He understood as no one in the world ever had or could. Then he asked me, as a lover would seek a kiss, "May I look inside?" I knew what he meant with no further explanation. I cannot describe to you the sensation as he wandered through the innermost secrets of my life and thoughts. It was spiritual, exquisitely painful, exalting, and through it all, there was a feeling of coming together that transcended any experience I had ever shared with anyone, ever. It was beyond sex, beyond love. When it ended, I felt like a physically deformed person, somehow miraculously made whole and sound. My only sadness and pain was at the knowledge that it was all over. I saw with new eyes. I also knew that there could never again be any relationship with another person that could touch me so.

GROSSMAN: Philadelphia was shortly after that, wasn't it?

SOKOLOW: Yes. It's why I stopped our relationship, Martin. I knew then that I would devote the rest of my life to being near to and helping Eddie where I could, and praying that there would be some useful way I could continue to share his company.

HENSKEY: Then you were in love with him?

SOKOLOW: As Magdalene loved Christ, yes. But in other ways, I became his confidante. You see, as he grew into his powers, he began to drift away from the company of men. His inquiries into what he was, and why, began to take him further and further into abstract ideas and reasoning. I became his sounding board; a foot on the ground. I had seen him through his various states of development. While he was at school, at least once a month, I would fly to Chicago and we'd be together for a day, sometimes two.

CASE: You were lovers, then?

SOKOLOW: Please excuse me for laughing, Mr. Case. The sensations I have described to you so completely transcend any small inkling you may have of relationships between two people. It bears the same relationship to sex that sex does to lunch. But one may do without lunch. I could not do without the joining we had.

HENSKEY: You would have done anything to maintain the relationship?

SOKOLOW: Within the limits of my personal ethical code, yes. No, I retract that. Yes, I would have done anything: lied, cheated, stolen, betrayed. Perhaps even killed to keep him. The exquisitely beautiful part of it all was that I knew he would never have asked me to do such things. Even now, I wonder what I should do, if he needed me.

HENSKEY: He's beyond such needs now.

SOKOLOW: He has been beyond such needs for six weeks.

HENSKEY: I don't know what you mean.

SOKOLOW: How could you? I barely grasp it myself, and I have seen him developing toward this point. Shared his thoughts. Why do you think you could never keep track of him? How did he go from country to country at will? How did he manipulate the money systems of four countries?

HENSKEY: That's what we're here to find out.

SOKOLOW: First, he is completely telepathic. He can not only read your thoughts, but can make you think, feel, see what he wants. The day Mr. Case was in my office, Eddie wanted Case to see the girl he saw. The girl was Eddie to all who saw him but me. To me, he was Eddie. He could board any flight to any country in the world and be unseen, or be seen as he wanted to be seen. If he chose, no one would remember seeing anyone.

He is a complete psychokinetic. He could, once he had been to a place, return there without any vehicle other than his mind.

He is clairvoyant. He can predict the future up to two or three weeks. Not just general trends. Particulars: the money market, the stock exchange, horse races.

CASE: My God!

SOKOLOW: Closer to that than your remark would seem, Mr. Case. About six weeks ago, the remodeling that the "visitor" had done to Eddie was complete. The "visitor" took the chance of driving his new home hopelessly insane. It made itself known to him.

HENSKEY: And?

SOKOLOW: I'm not sure. Once he knew what had happened to him, Eddie arranged for me to meet him.

He established rapport with me and allowed me to learn all I now know. It took less than ten seconds. Then he left saying that he would be in touch with me. He had one more project he wanted to try.

CASE: Which was?

SOKOLOW: The complete merging of the "visitor" and his own psyche. And one step further. He wanted to attempt the separation process that the "visitor" was incapable of doing alone. He would then no longer be bound to his body and could move through time and space at will.

CASE: And died in the failed attempt.

GROSSMAN: If what I'm thinking is so, I think not.

SOKOLOW: Quite right, Martin. He didn't fail. He succeeded!

HENSKEY: Then you mean to tell me that he's now floating around somewhere in time or space, looking for his future cousins?

SOKOLOW: Not at all. He's right here in your precious, secure headquarters. All you destroyed with your autopsy was the shell he had vacated. He can occupy or seem to occupy any body shell he so desires. At present, you know him as your Agent Ortiz.

HENSKEY: Case! Get on the horn. Find Ortiz and put him under guard! What the hell are you waiting for?

CASE: I already know where he is. We're too late.

HENSKEY: You didn't give him a day's leave, did you? I wanted him to stay on the base!

CASE: I'm afraid it's worse than that. I gave him the whole damn national security system for a toy. I gave him clearance to the ODIN complex!

YOU'RE RIGHT, CASE BABY. IT'S ONE HELLUVA SWELL TOY. DON'T BOTHER WITH THE GUARDS. YOUR

INTERCOM WON'T WORK UNLESS I WANT IT TO. THE DOOR WORKS, THOUGH. WHY DON'T YOU COME ON DOWNSTAIRS AND WE'LL HAVE A LITTLE TALK?

GEORGE CASE

Henskey keeps his cool under fire. I have to admit it. When the message from NIETZSCHE came over the intercom in the interrogation room, I nearly panicked. Even when I told Henskey about giving Ortiz clearance for the ODIN complex, he didn't ask how or why. He accepted that it had been done and acted on it. He also had the presence of mind to answer NIETZSCHE in a matter-of-fact tone. "I'll join you immediately, Rodriguez. Just where downstairs are you?"

"HARD TO SAY, HENSKEY," came the voice over the intercom. "YOU COULD SAY THAT I AM THE DOWNSTAIRS. OR THAT I'M INSIDE ODIN. ONCE I SAW THE SETUP, I WAS PRETTY SURE I COULD USE IT THE WAY I DID ORTIZ. AFTER ALL, ODIN HAS A SORT OF LIFE. IT MEETS ALL THE REQUIREMENTS, PLUS A FEW BONUSES. BY THE WAY, NO REMARKS TO ANY GUARDS ON THE WAY DOWN. I CAN HEAR ANYTHING YOU SAY. I HAVE YOUR MAN, ORTIZ, SO IF YOU WANT TO LOSE HIM, ONE WRONG WORD IS ALL IT TAKES. UNDERSTAND?"

"I read you. I'll come to the main data console, then?"

"GOOD. AND BRING CASE, GROSSMAN, AND MYRA WITH YOU."

We found Ortiz downstairs. He was sitting in front of the main display console. But so far as Ortiz was concerned, it could have been a blank slab of concrete. He was playing with the buttons on his Cardincut blazer. A fine line of drool ran from a corner of his mouth and into his lap. As we came into the room, he looked up for a second. The blank look in his eyes still haunts me. Then he went back to his game with his coat buttons. Sokolow and Grossman went over to him immediately.

"What do you think, Myra?" asked Grossman.

Sokolow examined him. "Without instruments, difficult to say. Knowing what we know, I'd say shock and withdrawal. How permanent, or if any real damage has been done, it would be foolish to guess. The best person to ask would be Eddie."

I glanced over at the series of panels studded with illuminated dials and pilot lights that was the main display console. It comprised the iceberg tip of the huge ODIN complex. How do you talk to a machine? The answer was quick coming.

"HE'LL RECOVER. YOU REALLY OUGHT TO BRIEF YOUR MEN, HENSKY. I ONLY DAMAGED HIM A BIT BECAUSE HE DIDN'T KNOW WHAT WAS GOING ON. WHEN I TOOK OVER, HE THOUGHT HE WAS GOING INSANE."

Henskey approached the programming console. "All right, Rodriguez. I accept the fact that you control ODIN. What is it you want from us?"

"YOU'VE GOT IT ALL WRONG, HENSKEY. THERE'S NOT A THING IN THIS WORLD YOU CAN OFFER ME THAT I DON'T ALREADY HAVE. THE ONE THING I NEEDED WAS A BODY. YOU FOOLS DESTROYED MINE. BUT THIS ONE WILL DO JUST FINE. IN MANY WAYS, IT'S EVEN BETTER THAN WHAT I HAD. IT DIDN'T TAKE LONG TO GET USED TO TRANSISTORS INSTEAD OF NERVES; SERVO-MECHANISMS FOR MUSCLES. AND NOW I HAVE EARS AND EYES IN EVERY PLACE YOU HAVE A LISTEN-

ING OR MONITORING DEVICE. I CAN BE HERE AND IN LOS ANGELES AT THE SAME TIME IF I WANT. AND OH, ALL THE LOVELY INFORMATION YOUR AGENCY HAS STORED HERE IN THE MEMORY BANKS, FELIX, BABY."

"Felix?" I said aloud.

"SURE, FELIX," said the ODIN speakers. "I'M SUR-PRISED AT YOU, CASE. DIDN'T YOU KNOW THAT HEN-SKEY'S MIDDLE NAME IS FELIX?"

He had me there. In the twenty years that I had known Henskey, I knew his middle initial was "F," but I never knew it stood for Felix.

ODIN/Eddie continued, "THAT'S NOTHING. I KNOW THE COMPLETE LIFE STORY OF EVERYONE WHO WORKS FOR I.G.O., PLUS THE WHOLE DOSSIERS ON ANYONE THEY'VE EVER KEPT A FILE ON. WOULD YOU LIKE TO KNOW THE REASON YOU'VE NEVER BEEN PROMOTED PAST A GRADE EIGHT, CASE? REMEMBER THOSE SWELL AFTERNOONS YOU SPENT WITH YOUR ENGLISH LIT. PROFESSOR?"

I felt a cold trickle of sweat run down my back. It hadn't been anything, really. I mean, kids do get crushes on instructors. I had idolized Brother Paul. And nothing actually happened. But there were a lot of snide rumors. What made it worse was that Brother Paul had been transferred not too long after. But I had no idea it was in my personnel file!

"WHAT'S THE MATTER, CASE? YOU'RE AWFULLY QUIET. WHY DON'T YOU TELL ALL THE NICE PEOPLE ABOUT YOUR GAY, GAY COLLEGE DAYS?"

I stood there, unable to say a word. The machine-driven voice went on, "OH, AND THE REALLY CHOICE THINGS I COULD TELL YOU ABOUT HENSKEY. WOULD YOU LIKE TO HEAR HOW HE THREW YOUR BUDDY, O'HANLON, TO THE WOLVES IN EAST GERMANY? HE COULD HAVE SAVED HIM, YOU KNOW. HE . . ."

"What's the purpose of all this, Rodriguez?" cut in Henskey.

"NO PURPOSE AT ALL, HENSK. OTHER THAN IT AMUSES ME TO SEE YOU SQUIRM. AND I CAN'T THINK OF A NICER PERSON TO MAKE SQUIRM. IF IT COMES TO THAT, I DON'T NEED TO HAVE REASONS FOR ANYTHING I DO. THAT I WANT TO DO THEM IS ENOUGH. IF IT AMUSED ME, I COULD SEND A FLIGHT OF NUCLEAR MISSILES AT MOSCOW RIGHT NOW. IT WOULD TAKE NO MORE EFFORT THAN LIFTING A FINGER, IF I HAD FINGERS TO LIFT. WOULD YOU LIKE ME TO SHOW YOU?"

"In the name of God, Rodriguez!" said Henskey. "What is it you want? One doesn't make threats without wanting something. There has to be something!"

"YOU SAID IT, HENSK," came the voice through the speakers. "BUT NOT QUITE THE RIGHT WAY. IT'S IN THE NAME OF GOD RODRIGUEZ. AND FROM HERE ON, THAT'S THE WAY IT'S GOING TO BE. I'M YOUR GOD. WHY NOT? I SEE ALL, HEAR ALL, KNOW ALL, IF I CHOOSE, I CAN DESTROY THE ENTIRE WORLD BY NUCLEAR FIRE, FOR I AM A JEALOUS AND VENGEFUL GOD. THIS IS MY TEMPLE, WHERE YOU WILL COME TO WORSHIP. YOU CAN KNEEL BEFORE ME, HENSKEY. BECAUSE ALTHOUGH I MAY NOT BE YOUR MAKER, I CAN CERTAINLY BE YOUR DESTROYER. I SAID KNEEL!"

"Go to hell, Rodriguez," said Henskey through his teeth.

A series of red lights began to flash on the data console, and a persistant beep-beep tone started.

"ALL RIGHT, HENSKEY. YOU KNOW THE SOUND. INSTALLATION TWENTY-SIX IN ALASKA IS ARMED AND READY TO FLY. SIXTEEN COBALT WARHEAD MISSILES AIMED DIRECTLY AT RED SQUARE. IF YOU AREN'T ON YOUR KNEES BEFORE ME IN TEN SECONDS, MOSCOW

GETS IT. AND THAT MEANS THAT BEFORE THEY EVER LAND THERE, AS MANY WILL BE AIMED AT NEW YORK, CHICAGO, AND L.A. I SAID KNEEL!"

And there, in the sub-basement of I.G.O. headquarters in Greenglade, Maryland, the director of operations for half the country knelt before the god he had helped to make. Sokolow and Grossman stood unmoving, on either side of Ortiz, Sokolow with her hand resting lightly on the poor kid's shoulder. As Henskey knelt before the flashing panels, she left her position and advanced toward the console. I couldn't read any expression on her face as she came up alongside where Henskey was kneeling. As she drew abreast of Henskey, she, too, sank to her knees. Lights blinked on the display.

"NO, NO. NOT YOU, MYRA," said the mechanical voice. "FROM NOW ON, THEY WILL KNEEL TO YOU AS WELL. YOU WILL BE MY PRIESTESS AND CONSORT. ANYONE WHO SEEKS MY BENEFICENCE MUST BEG IT THROUGH YOU."

The thing that was ODIN/Eddie laughed. The speakers for the ODIN complex had been set up for voice response. But machines don't laugh. I can't describe the sound that came through it. But I'll remember it to the day I die. I've heard it since, many times, and it never fails to curdle my insides.

Sokolow got to her feet and said in a quiet voice, "Anything you wish, Eddie. May I still call you that?"

"YOU, AND ONLY YOU. PERHAPS, RAFAEL. TO THE REST OF THE WORLD, I AM LORD GOD, EDUARDO, THE FIRST AND LAST. INSIDE THIS SHELL, THIS MACHINE, WHICH EVEN NOW I AM IMPROVING, THE WORLD IS MINE. A NEW WORLD IS BEGINNING. IT WILL BE A NEW, BETTER WORLD. WITHOUT HUNGER, WITHOUT

DISEASE, FOR I CAN HEAL. I HAVE DISCOVERED THE GLUE THAT HOLDS THE UNIVERSE TOGETHER! DID YOU KNOW, FOR INSTANCE, MYRA, THAT ALL CANCER IS CAUSED BY IMPROPER ENERGY EXCHANGE WITHIN THE INTERNAL STRUCTURE OF DNA MOLECULES? I CAN ERADICATE IT. DID YOU KNOW THAT BY THE SAME PROCESS, I CAN REVERSE DAMAGE DONE TO MINDS AND BODIES? I CAN GENERATE NEW TISSUE. IF I CHOOSE, I CAN RAISE THE DEAD! AND YOU, MYRA, THE FRIGHTENED LITTLE GIRL ON THAT DAY IN DACHAU . . . YOU WILL BE THE ONE TO WHOM THE WORLD WILL BEG FOR MY BLESSINGS. YOU WILL BE THE QUEEN OF ALL CREATION!"

The little, birdlike woman seemed to grow visibly taller. She turned to Grossman and me and favored us with a wintry smile. "Welcome to the first day of the reign of Eduardo the First and Last," she said.

DARRYL HENSKEY

Sokolow is amazing. If someone had just given me the world on a platter, I don't know what I would have done. Whatever it might have been, I wasn't ready for her response. It was as though somebody had told her she looked well, or complimented her on a new hairdo. Took it completely in her stride.

Once Rodriguez ordered us out of the ODIN complex, she became her previous unruffled self. I was in a flap, naturally. I couldn't touch her for judas goating us all, but the first thing I did was to start drawing up charges against Case for letting Ortiz/NIETZSCHE into the ODIN complex. I didn't even order quarters for Sokolow and Grossman. I was dictating particulars before I was even fully seated at my desk . . . but she stopped me with a question. "Why do you wish to punish Mr. Case for your own error in judgment, Mr. Henskey? And what makes you think you still have the authority to do so?"

I didn't miss the look on Case's face when she said it, either. "You heard what Rodriguez . . ."

"Eduardo the First and Last."

"Whatever. You heard what he said. Until he has his interview with the President, we are to act as if nothing unusual has happened. If that's so, while I still have a scrap of authority left, I'm going to nail Case's ass to my office door for this."

"I think not," she said. "You forget that I am liaison between Eduardo and the government at this point. And inasmuch as Eduardo has the power to destroy you all, I should think twice about punishing the man who made it possible. You don't want to anger Eduardo, do you?"

She turned to Case. "It also might be that you will one day become a saint, Mr. Case. That is, if Eduardo is God."

The voice came over the intercom at my desk. "YOU DON'T REALLY DOUBT THAT I AM, DO YOU, MYRA?"

I jumped a foot. I'd forgotten that every room in HQ is linked to the ODIN monitoring system. The voice went on, "I SEE ALL AND HEAR ALL. L REWARD THE FAITHFUL. I CAN PUNISH THE UNWORTHY. OBSERVE!"

The lights in the room died. I groped my way to the door in the dark. It was on security-lock from the switch at my desk. But my console was dark, too.
were trapped. Then I noticed the momentary si-
in the room. He'd cut off the air!

Top security offices like mine are nearly perfectly soundproofed. To do that, they must be sealed tight. Conditioned air enters the room through a series of acoustic baffles. When the air is cut off, there's no other way for the air to get in. It may have been my imagination, but already, the room seemed stuffy.

What threw me was Grossman's reaction. He went off his head. He started screaming and clawing at the walls, the furniture; falling down. He grabbed me, at one point, but I managed to get loose. Abruptly, the lights came on again, and the air began sighing through the vents. Grossman collapsed on the floor, sobbing.

"Eddie, Eddie," said Sokolow in a gentle voice. "You know from his file that Martin is a claustrophobe. Surely, you could have chosen some other way to make your point with Mr. Henskey."

"CAN YOU THINK OF A BETTER WAY THAN TO LOCK SOMEONE UP IN A DARK, AIRLESS ROOM WITH A MADMAN? BESIDES, GROSSMAN ISN'T HURT. I READ ALL HIS BODY FUNCTIONS AS RETURNING TO NORMAL. YES, HE'S COMING OUT OF IT NOW."

He was right. Grossman was sitting up and beginning to collect himself. Sokolow went over and comforted him. Once she saw he was all right, she came over and returned her attention to me.

"Mr. Henskey, I think it best that we all sit down and calmly discuss how to carry out Eduardo's wishes. There is no escape, nor any deception possible. This interview with the President. You have the authority to set it up?"

"Not over the phone. The President, as a matter of policy, never comes to Greenglade. We report to him through the Secretary of Defense. Hardly ever in person. I've met the Secretary once, and I've never met the President."

"Then the rules must be broken. Eduardo wishes the President to come here, therefore he must."

"Easily said. But I can't just pick up the phone and say, 'Mr. President, drop what you're doing and get your tail over to Greenglade on the double.' I don't think I could even convince him on the phone that what's going on is for real. I'd have to get an appointment with the Secretary, and through him, reach the President. I could probably get the Secretary at home right now. But I'd have to see the President personally to get him to come here."

"Then that is how we shall do it," said Sokolow.

"How?" I put in. "Eduardo the First won't let us leave Greenglade!"

"YOU HAVE OUR PERMISSION TO SEE THE PRESIDENT, HENSKEY. MYRA WILL ACCOMPANY YOU. BUT AS YOU SPEAK TO HIM, REMEMBER THE MISSILES."

On the way over to the White House in the agency limousine, Sokolow said nothing at all. I though she was in some sort of brown study. Once, when I asked her about Ortiz, all she said was, "Eddie says he will be all right." So, naturally, I was surprised when after the limo had cleared the gate and pulled up at the side entrance to the White House, she motioned me not to go right in. We got out and stood to one side.

"Quickly, Mr. Henskey. I would not speak in the automobile because I assumed that like everything else your agency owns, it is connected to that computer."

"It is," I admitted.

"So, we must act before he suspects. You realize he has become unbalanced. We must somehow remove him from that all-powerful machine of yours and get him some help. No. Don't speak. Listen.

100

Something must have happened when Eddie's host body was destroyed. His mind . . . I don't know. When he began to speak as he did, I realized that this no longer was the person I adored. It was someone, something different . . . evil. I believe he is capable of making good his threats of destruction. Our only hope to help him is to trick him."

"Trick him?" I gasped. "A super-genius who outthought the agency, swindled its counterpart in three major western nations, took over ODIN, and can read minds. How the hell do you propose to do it?"

Sokolow actually smiled; "You should trust your machines less and your own senses more, Mr. Case. I noticed immediately. Since he has occupied that monster computer of yours, he hasn't read anyone's thoughts. If he had, I wouldn't be here talking to you. He has somehow modified the polygraph system and is keeping tabs on us that way. With a monitor in every area of the Agency and God knows where else, he doesn't have to read thoughts. I told you something went wrong when he entered a host that wasn't a human body. He's lost some of his powers.

"I realized this when he began to speak to us in that basement room. Had he read my thoughts then, I would not be here now. But tell me, is the White House monitored as well? I read that all listening devices there had been removed."

At the time, I was glad the light was poor where we were standing. I'm sure I turned red. "No, dammit," I replied. "They're still in there. We made a show of taking out the ones that report to the President. We had to. You remember the big stink in the papers about it. But the other ones, the ones tied in to ODIN, are still in place."

Sokolow sighed deeply. "Then we must follow Eddie's instructions exactly. He will be listening to all we say. There is no time now to plan, but I enjoy Eddie's confidence for the present. I'll try to find a way for us to speak again, soon. We must go inside now, before Eddie becomes suspicious."

As we entered the White House, I began putting my mind to the task before me. All I had to do was explain to the President how I had turned over control of the western world to an insane Puerto Rican slum kid who thought he was God.

The New York Times

Subject of Presidential Television Address Still Undisclosed

WASHINGTON, June 20—Rumors are circulating that the subject of the forthcoming television address by the President will bear on the unusual events of the past two weeks on Capitol Hill.

A blanket of silence has enveloped the White House since the President vetoed the controversial Clark-Michaels Bill, calling for severe cutbacks in Public Works projects as well as elimination of most aid to the disadvantaged.

Party leaders were at a loss to explain the President's actions on the Clark-Michaels Bill, in view of the fact that it was initiated at the suggestion of the President himself.

The television address is scheduled for this Friday at 8:00 P.M. and will be carried by all major networks.

DARRYL HENSKEY

I guess Rodriguez figures he's home free, now. The President is going to make it official on Friday. I don't know why Rodriguez wants to make it public that he's been running the country for the past two weeks. Everything is going the way he wants it; no one knows he's doing it but a handful of high officials. He hasn't made any sweeping changes. Just some small items here and there. The only thing that made waves was the Clark-Michaels veto. I think that Rodriguez has been studying and consolidating his strength.

I thought that the first thing he'd do was start dissolving the Agency. After all, knowing what we do, we're the only threat to his plans. Maybe he figures he can keep us blackmailed into silence indefinitely. But if he's having it made public on Friday, his plans must be nearly completed.

What gripes me most is that I have to keep maintaining appearances at his orders. Here I am, in complete control of all personnel and equipment of the I.G.O. headquarters, and I can't lift a finger to stop him. Every day, a new order for installation of surveillance equipment comes across my desk, and I have to rubber-stamp it approved. I think by now, he has eyes and ears in every major agency and private firm in the country. Talk about Big Brother.

The decoration for Ortiz came through yesterday. Not that it means a thing to him, poor kid. He's no better off than he was two weeks ago. Sokolow thinks that Rodriguez is keeping him that way on purpose. After all, we did destroy Rodriguez's body with that autopsy. Sokolow feels that Ortiz is there to be used like a spare part. She may be right. Physically, he's healthy enough. Mentally, he's a turnip. I wish that Sokolow wouldn't take the chances she does in communicating with me. She slips me these notes when we're out of range of Rodriguez's video monitors. But there are new ones going in each day. In a few days, there won't be a corner of the entire Greenglade compound that won't be visible to him. There must be some way to get him out of the ODIN!

GEORGE CASE

Screwed again! If I don't get out of this building soon, I'm going to go buggier than Rodriguez. At least today, I got as far as the loading platform in Area A. Who'd have thought he'd have a video monitor on trucks to the garbage dump? I've showered twice, and I still smell like a kitchen gone rancid. If that wasn't bad enough, I had to hear his lecture and that horrid laugh. If Sokolow hadn't intervened. I would have gone around smelling like a garbage truck indefinitely. He thought it was funny that I would have been a health hazard if I didn't get cleaned up.

The hell of the situation is that nobody can make any plans to get him out of the ODIN. The only ones who know are prisoners, one way or another. The President is a virtual prisoner in the White House, and Rodriguez has the place filled with more bugs than a Jersey swamp.

Thank God he trusts Sokolow. She, at least, has freedom of the compound. I know she's been passing notes to Henskey. She's taking a helluva chance each time she does it. I don't know if even she can do anything, but if I give up that hope, I might as well lie down and die.

She spends at least five hours a day in the data display room with Rodriguez. What they talk about or what they do, we can only guess. She's the only one with access to the room now. Anyone who wants to get near the ODIN has to be cleared through her. Oh, we go through the motions. Technically, access to the ODIN is signed by Henskey. But at this point, he can't even go to the john without Rodriguez's OK through Sokolow. I hope Henskey or someone on the White House staff can come up with something. I'm completely up a tree.

I know it's a silly point, but I hope that if we get out of this mess, it's hushed up. It's bad enough being the man responsible for it happening. But my punishment for trying to get out through the garbage is worse. Rodriguez has passed the word that in the future I am to be referred to in print and addressed as "Stinky."

RAFAEL GUZMAN

I knew Eddie would come through! They still won't let me out of here, but man, you'd think I was the king of the world the way they treat me. I talked to Pablo on the phone today. Didn't have to pay any long distance, either. I can call anyone, anywhere in the world if I want.

I got this great apartment with a picture window on the second floor. The second floor is the top floor in this joint. They got six floors below ground, but only two above.

Two weeks ago, they had me way downstairs in one room with a bed, a sink, and a john. No light switches inside. There wasn't even a handle on my side of the door. Now I got a phone, a color TV, wall-to-wall carpet, a bedroom, a kitchen, and a living room. Real class. What I don't understand is why I can't see Eddie. I get notes from him, all typed out, but no one will even tell me where he is. Something's going on. I think Eddie's got something on somebody in the government. Especially since Pablo got the check in the mail.

When I talked to him on the phone, he was real excited. Three days ago, when he picked up the mail, there was a check made out to Papa. It was one of those blue government checks with the holes in it. For twenty-five hundred bucks! No letter with it, just the check. Pablo says it was from Social Security, and that it was marked for total disability. Well it's for sure Papa is disabled since the heart attack. But when we asked about it two years ago, they brushed us off at that social security office downtown. I think Eddie must be behind it. He always said that there's a lot of benefits that uptown people could have, if they only knew about them.

Anyway, I still want to get out of here. I know I shouldn't complain, but even if it's got wall-to-wall and TV, a slam is still a slam. If only I could get in touch with Eddie. I mean, see him face to face. I want to go home. I wonder what Lydia Prieto is doing right now?

DARRYL HENSKEY

Hope! Maybe a slight chance, but there's hope! Sokolow slipped me a note under the table at lunch today. I had to stay cool and finish the meal before I could look at it in the john, then flush it.

Case, Grossman, Sokolow, and I eat separately nowadays. We have a table at the commissary that no one can approach except to serve us our meals—part of Rodriguez's incommunicado plan. I think he gets a kick out of watching us eat and not being able to talk about the one thing that's on all our minds. It's at mealtimes that Sokolow gives us the word from on high. The latest from Eduardo the First. I don't know how she is managing this double game of hers. There's no doubt that Rodriguez has us outthought at every turn.

Had to laugh at Case today, in spite of myself. Sitting there smelling like a goat in heat. Rodriguez caught him trying to get out of the compound in a garbage truck, then wouldn't let him clean up. I'll never forget the look on his face when Sokolow told us everybody had to call him "Stinky" from now on. He's lucky, really. Rodriguez could just as easily have had him done away with for that stunt. But crazy or not, there's nothing wrong with Rodriguez's judgment as an administrator. Killing Case for trying to escape would have made him a martyr. Making him a laughingstock is a better example.

I was so wrapped up in wondering about the note Sokolow gave me, that I barely noticed what she had to say. For the past two weeks at meals, the pronouncements from Rodriguez have been mostly about the way we are to act and speak. They don't have to do with any of his tactical plans. Nobody knows what they are, not even Sokolow.

I was brought up short when Sokolow asked me if there would be any diplomatic difficulty implementing Rodriguez's latest order to the troops. Eduardo the First's latest whim is cultural. He wants a command performance by Alberto Noriga in the compound theater. Noriga is in town for his annual concert and White House appearance. Under any other set of circumstances, I'd be delighted to hear him myself. I keep meaning to get tickets whenever he comes to town, but with the Agency to run, I somehow never get to it. When Ellen was alive, it was different. We made a regular thing of seeing him. Funny, she used to keep telling me each year that we had to see him because there was no telling how much longer he'd be able to play. He was in his late sixties, then. He must be in his seventies, now, and he's outlived my poor, dear Ellen.

Those old country guys must have such a grip on life. I'm fifty-five, now, and for most of my life, Noriga has been acknowledged as the world's greatest classical guitarist. I hope I can keep my mind on the performance. Sokolow's note said "Sit next to me at the concert. I have a plan."

INTERIM REPORT: EYES ONLY

To: Darryl F. Henskey, District Supervisor, I.G.O. HQ, Greenglade, MD.

From: Office of the Secretary of Defense

Re: Alberto Noriga

Henskey:

Arrangements have been made for Noriga to perform at the HQ theater at the Greenglade compound. As you know, Noriga is an old man and must restrict the number of performances he does each year. Under the circumstances, the President is taking a pass on the command performance at the White House. Noriga will have dinner with the President but will not perform. After dinner, he will be brought by limo to Greenglade. God only knows what Protocol gave his people as a reason. Happily, his country is one of the few left that feels they have to please us. Between us, I don't think it's a hardship on the President. It's my impression he's more a country and western music fan, anyway.

MARTIN GROSSMAN

Magnificent, simply magnificent. I've never seen Noriga perform, though I have many of his recordings. The Greenglade theater isn't really a concert hall. It's set up for showing motion picture films, and I understand from Henskey it converts to a war room if such a contingency arises.

I wonder what the old man made of it all. An audience of four, plus his entourage. The real audience, he never saw. But he certainly heard Rodriguez. It was after he had finished playing the Segovia transcription of Bach's *Chaconne in D*. I have the recording at home, and I've played it many times. But somehow, hearing a recording is different from actually seeing the man perform it. One becomes accustomed to the tricks and effects that emanate from a stereo record player. After a few years' time of only mechanically reproduced music, the mind no longer associates a living performer with the music. It becomes still another thing done for us by machines, another part of the electronic alienation

110

of our society. Despite the circumstances that keep me here, I was enchanted by the sight and sound of one old man and an even older guitar. It was therefore thoughtless of Rodriguez to do what he did.

When Noriga had finished the *Chaconne,* which is very demanding, Myra stood up after the applause and spoke to him from the audience. She actually told him what his encore was to be! Unthinkable to an artist of Noriga's stature. He was bewildered, of course. The piece she requested was the *Filiberto Opus 16.*

The old man sat there for a moment and then replied in heavily accented English, "Is madam aware that the *Filiberto 16* is a guitar concerto?"

I'm sure Myra didn't know. Her taste has always run to piano, particularly Chopin. Whatever she replied was lost, though. The voice of Eduardo the First came through the theater sound system, then. I don't know enough Spanish to practice my profession in the language, but I understood what came through the speakers:

"PLEASE PLAY AS REQUESTED, MAESTRO. THE ORCHESTRA WILL BE PROVIDED."

Noriga looked around momentarily for the source of the voice, then said, "I do not see an orchestra, and Noriga does not play with recorded accompaniment."

"WE WOULD NOT OFFEND NORIGA WITH RECORDED ACCOMPANIMENT. THE ORCHESTRA IS COMPLETELY ELECTRONIC AND UNDER MY CONTROL IN ANOTHER PART OF THE THEATER. IF YOU DOUBT, LISTEN."

The opening strains of the *Filiberto 16* came through the house system. It's an ambitious work, filled with orchestral fireworks. Many critics have disapproved of the work itself, but all have gone along with it because of the fantastic job Noriga does on it. It was written for him, and is one of the few major symphonic works by a Puerto Rican composer that is performed on a regular basis. I have the recording with Filiberto himself conducting. The music swept and swirled.

"DO YOU HEAR, MAESTRO?" said the voice from the speakers. "I CAN VARY TEMPI TO SUIT YOU. YOU HAVE BUT TO PLAY, IF YOU WILL."

It must be Noriga's flexibility of mind that keeps him young at his age. He listened intently for a few minutes to the sound of the orchestra from the speakers, then said, "It is good. Noriga will play."

And play he did. I have my own thoughts as to what should or could be done about Eduardo Rodriguez. But there is music in his madness. I've played *Filiberto 16* many times, and even the composer didn't conduct with the feeling, the style, the grace of the electronic *thing* five floors below us. At one point, I reached over to take Myra's hand, but she sat there between Henskey and me, completely rapt. I could see that even Henskey was touched. He sat stock still, barely breathing throughout the performance. There may be more to Henskey than I thought.

DARRYL HENSKEY

I sat through the first part of the program on pins and needles, waiting for Sokolow to pass me a note. Nothing. After a while, I figured something had
112

gone wrong, and that there was no point in doing anything but listening to Noriga. I thought it might be coming when she stood up and talked to the old man from the audience, but still no go. After the byplay with Rodriguez over the sound system, I sat there waiting for it to be over. A few minutes into the piece, I heard her say, "Henskey! No, don't move. Don't act in any way as though you are doing anything but listening to the music. His attention is occupied just now, but he is perfectly capable of monitoring the entire building while doing what he is doing. Don't try to reply to me, either. Think of your answer, no more. I will hear you."

I nearly fell off my chair. Sokolow wasn't speaking! From the corner of my eye, I could see that her lips hadn't moved. I thought to myself, "What the hell is this?"

"The time I have been spending with Eduardo has not been in vain. I have convinced him that he is vulnerable now that he can only read responses on the polygraph. He believed me when I told him he needs a telepath to monitor others' thoughts. He has taught me the process!"

I must have been all upside the wall. Her thoughts came cutting through the jumble of anxiety and relief in my head at that moment. "Please, Henskey. Get control of yourself. This process is new to me. When you are excited this way, there is neither order nor reason to your thought patterns. It's as though you were screaming in my ears."

"Sorry. How's this?"

"Much better. We have very little time. I want you to review in your mind, very slowly and methodically, all you know of this matter. What you know that Eduardo has done to take over."

I did what she asked as best I could. It was hard. My conscience kept nagging at me with each piece of top priority information I reviewed in my mind. I've made a career of keeping secrets. In order to tell her what Rodriguez had done, I had to tell her the whole works: How I.G.O. is organized, locations of installations, identities of key personnel, all that I had sworn I would give up my very life to conceal.

Once I had done that, she said, "Now tell me of the ODIN machine. Think of all you know about it. No detail, no matter how small or inconsequential-seeming, must you omit."

Mentally gritting my teeth, I did it. When I had finished, her voice again said inside my head, "Very good, Mr. Henskey. By the way, you are right in thinking that now that I know, I am as great a threat as Eddie is. You may comfort yourself in knowing that regardless of the consequences of your actions, you can be in no worse a situation than before."

The music came to an end with a flashy finish. While the last notes were still hanging in the air, I heard her inside my mind. "I must review what you have given me. When we have breakfast tomorrow, create some kind of diversion. I will try to communicate with you then."

I didn't get much sleep.

RAFAEL GUZMAN

Going home tomorrow! Just got another one of those typewriter notes from Eddie. He says that after Friday, nothing that's happened is gonna matter

114

anymore. Easy to say. I remember when the Barons got busted. For a year after, any time some window got broken, the man was on us. Once they got your name, babe, you better be ready to see them all the time.

And the bust with the Barons was just a protest. This is different. What with finding that dead guy in Greenberg's old pad, it could even be a murder rap. Maybe me and Pablo can sell the business and move. I never been to Puerto Rico. Pablo was born there, and he knows all the lines. Yeah, if it gets too heavy uptown with the fuzz, we could go to P.R.

What knocks me out is the treatment I been getting since Eddie sent the first note to me. The marine guard down the hall calls me Mr. Guzman. I could get used to that.

I guess it's for real they're letting me go. That marine up the hall just came and brought me a box of brand-new clothes. I been wearing Marine Corps dungarees since they picked me up. My other clothes got pretty screwed up when they started pushing me around. I bet Eddie picked these things out. He knows my sizes and all. You should see these vines. A suit with a vest! Even brand-new underwear and socks.

I put on all the stuff and checked myself out in the mirror. The dude looking back at me from the mirror could go anywhere. Really. I look downtown enough to go dancing at the Waldorf Astoria. If they dance there. Could you dig them dancing *salsa* at the Waldorf?

GEORGE CASE

If I ever get out of this alive, Henskey is going to answer for this morning. Or maybe this whole business has sent him around the bend. He started in on me at breakfast and wouldn't quit. I've never seen him like this. True, he's always been a sarcastic bastard, but only when he feels somebody has let him down.

Maybe I should revise all my thinking about Henskey. If what Rodriguez said about O'Hanlon in Berlin is true, he's not the man I though he was. It's funny, but I can't work for a man I don't respect. I got those uncertain feelings about O'Hanlon just before he was shot crossing the Berlin Wall—from the wrong side. He'd been under Henskey's special orders all along. And Henskey just let them kill him. Like you'd toss away a Kleenex.

It's one thing to know that your life is on the line for your country. That's part of the job, and we all take risks. But it's something else to know that you can go at the hands of your own boss. I may be old-fashioned, or even naïve, but I just couldn't take it this morning.

We were having breakfast when Henskey got there. Grossman was talking to Sokolow. All he wants to talk about is this "future society" that's going to happen God-knows-when. He even takes notes. I don't know why he bothers. He's got a memory I'd give anything for. He can tell you verbatim anything he's ever read. Can tell you where and when he read it, too. What an agent he'd make! Inside man, naturally.

So no sooner had Henskey come to the table, when he starts in with the "Stinky" business. I know that Rodriguez did it to make an object lesson out of my escape try. But usually, we avoid addressing each other by name. I appreciate it; spares my feelings a bit. Oh, once in a while, Sokolow slips me a zinger. She still hasn't forgotten how I quiet-taped her that day at her office. Considering the influence she has with Rodriguez, I should be thankful she hasn't had me thrown into a cell downstairs.

But Henskey. I just couldn't take it. It was "Stinky" this and "Stinky" that. And "Do I smell something foul at this table?" He went at me like I was an enemy. I couldn't sit still anymore. I threw my tomato juice in his face. Funny, he just sat there. I was ready to take him apart if he'd have made a move. It was as though he wanted me to do it.

For a second, an embarrassing silence hung over the table. We all sat there, as if one word or move would have brought us down like a house of cards. Henskey sat there, with the tomato juice running down his face. He didn't even make a move to wipe it off. Just sat there. It was Grossman who broke the spell. He said in a quiet voice, "I think we're all under a strain. These outbursts and the baiting of Mr. Case don't help. I'm sure that Eduardo the First finds them amusing. Need we give him any more satisfaction?"

Henskey admitted he was out of line, then. I told him to forget it. He can. I won't. I have a few to settle with my boss. Before you could say it, the incident was over. Grossman was off again asking

117

Sokolow more about the future. I wonder what he's all about inside.

MARTIN GROSSMAN

Fascinated. I'm simply fascinated by this future society of Myra's. It appears to be a near-perfect social setup. After the incident between Case and Henskey this morning, she told me even more.

She explained to me how Eduardo can seem to assume any shape he desires. Seems that after a series of nuclear wars we will have, people won't look too much like people any more. Hard radiation plays hell with genetic structure. So among themselves, our future beings have agreed on an ideal appearance, which they project mentally. What Eduardo does is an offshoot of that process. Imagine a world where anyone can be what he wants, in appearance at least!

She also cleared up something that had been bothering me. I'd read that the future is made up of events directly built on what happens in the present. In other words, the future can be changed by what happens right now. I feared that what Eduardo is doing now may be screwing up the future, before it has a chance to happen. Myra laughed. "Martin," she said. "Don't you realize that these events are already part of the future? The changes Eduardo makes in history have occurred and been recorded. If you wish to be concerned about the future, I would suggest you follow Eduardo's instructions to the letter. We know that many of the changes that will occur will happen after a nuclear war. It may begin with us, here and now."

She's right, as usual. The future of man is secure. But this country and our culture may not be a part of it. We could end up like the Phoenicians, a footnote in history.

But if only we were free to investigate the full extent of Eduardo's paranormal powers. What a tool for healing! In psychiatry alone, years could be lopped off analysis with instant rapport.

And think of all those unfortunates whose lives are blighted by their physical appearances. Victims of birth defects, crippling diseases, accidents. They could appear as normal. Mutes could "speak" through telepathy. And it's all locked up inside Eduardo, who I am convinced has crossed the line into paranoia. Or he may have been there all along. Paranoiacs can fool analysts and often do.

Which brings me to another point: the future visitors as legend. Myra explains poltergeists, ghosts, and demonic possession as the improper merging of "visitors" with host bodies. I think she's missing an important and very persistant legend. As she describes this "coming together" with Eduardo, and her need for the act, I get chills. This relationship with a creature who can change shape, read thoughts, and compel others to obey has a name. I think of Eduardo leaving his body behind in a deathlike state, and it brings the name to mind: *vampirism!*

DARRYL HENSKEY

Hot flash from the White House. The President is coming over to HQ. He has to speak with Rodriguez. I bet he does. I don't envy the President his situation. For the past two weeks, without saying what's going on, he's been preparing for Friday. Tomorrow, he officially turns over the keys to Rodriguez. Domestic policy is one thing—martial law, federal control of communications and travel, troops to maintain order—it can be done. But foreign policy is something else.

I know from past dealings that the Russians don't believe half of what we say, even when we tell them the truth. That's what's stalled disarmament talks all these years. And even if we can convince the Russians we're legit, there's still the Red Chinese. They don't even believe the goddamn Russians!

I'd give a lot to know what Sokolow's plan is. I'd give still more to know if she's leading us down the primrose path again. I have only her word that she's had a change of heart about Rodriguez. She lied before. Good enough to fake out a polygraph. She could be lying now; asking me all I know of ODIN and the Agency to further Rodriguez's plans. But as she says, I can't be in any worse a spot.

The diversion at breakfast went well. After twenty years, I know where all Case's soft spots are. I pushed the right buttons, and he snapped. I thought for a second he was going to come across the table right after the tomato juice he threw in my face. I

120

tend to forget that George is an outside man and as such is very dangerous, physically. I'm so used to chewing these guys out and running them. But they are killers. George has taken out five of theirs and two of ours who have gone bad. He didn't lose any sleep over it, either.

During the diversion, Sokolow "asked" me about ODIN's power source. As if I hadn't been through it all over and over in my mind for two weeks. There's no way. The ODIN is powered by our own generators here in the Greenglade compound. The plant is one of the new mini-nuclear jobs. If the rest of the country went out, ODIN would still run for years. The nuke plant can't be shut down without clearance from me, the Secretary, and the President. And all that has to be filtered through ODIN, anyway. Which means Rodriguez. In essence, we can't turn off ODIN without ODIN's permission.

The only loophole I've seen is the emergency cutout. Sokolow was very interested in it. No go. The emergency cutout functions only if an unauthorized outsider tries to use any of the defense functions of the ODIN. But that's no longer in effect. Rodriguez armed and put a whole flight of nukes on standby. Saw him do it myself. If any outsider without the clearance had done that it would normally have triggered the cutout.

Sokolow wanted to know more about the cutout. It's a simple device. Even I understood when the engineering staff who installed it told me how it worked. If anyone without the clearance tries to use the ODIN, after a one minute wait, a power surge runs through the whole machine and fuses every circuit. No bombs, no blast, no danger to the rest of the HQ. Just *phttt!* And there goes one-hundred-twenty-five billion dollars worth of equipment. Once the cutout is turned on, it can't be turned off. Any tampering with the mechanism sets it in motion. But so what? Rodriguez has obviously bypassed the cutout. If he hadn't, the whole thing would have gone up as soon as he armed that flight of rockets at station twenty-six.

If Sokolow thinks she can find anything in the physical setup of ODIN that could get us off the hook, she'd better think again. I'm used up, myself. I've thought about it until my brain feels like used chewing gum.

No use bothering myself now, though. I have to set up security for a presidential visit. No President of the United States has ever visited Greenglade since it was built. There's no protocol set up for a president to come here. We have no place to put him, no regular honor guard. Well, if there's no precedent, I can't be called wrong on the way I handle it. I find it small comfort that this will be the first and last time it happens. After this, all orders will come from Greenglade and Rodriguez.

Should have known. Just got a memo from Eduardo the First. He's already got all security planned. Have to admit as I look it over, it's a masterpiece. Despite no one knowing that he exists, he's come up with a reasonable plan to relieve Secret Service of any responsibility once the President enters Greenglade. Our security takes over then. No one in the world could doubt our efficiency at Greenglade. Hell, we trained the Secret Service guys who guard the President, didn't we? Who could know that all our men answer to Rodriguez. They don't know that themselves!

Once this balloon goes up on Friday, I wonder

what I'm going to do? I've thought of killing myself. In ancient times, the king's bodyguard did that if they failed in their jobs. No denying I've failed. The rotten part of it all is that I can't shoot myself. I'd need Rodriguez's permission to requisition a gun to do it with.

GEORGE CASE

The President! What a joke. After all these years in the Agency, I've seen as much of the President as the average voter. TV, films; that's all. I drive past the White House and think, "There he is. In there. The man I take orders from; the man whose life I've sworn to protect. He wouldn't know who I was if I stepped on his foot."

He'll know who I am tonight, though. I can hear it all now. "Mr. President, you know Darryl Henskey. This is his assistant and number one field agent, Stinky." Christ! Rodriguez can't mean to have them call me that in front of the President. He can't! I have to talk to Sokolow. No use talking to Henskey.

MARTIN GROSSMAN

I have to rethink all I've set down in these notes. As I was having lunch with our little captive group, I glanced over at Myra. The thoughts I've had about the vampire legend came to mind. And as I looked directly at Myra she said to me, "It had occurred to me, this idea of yours. It may, in fact, be the basis for the legend. Please, Martin! Don't show any outward response to my words. As you can see, I am not actually speaking to you. You are receiving my thoughts."

Show a response? I was stunned. I couldn't have uttered a word. But as her words sank in, my heart gave a great leap. It meant that the talent, the paranormal abilities, could be acquired!

"Quite right, Martin," came the "voice" of Myra Sokolow. "It can and has been. It's not an involved process. Like Columbus and the mythical egg. Now that it has been done, everyone will wonder why it wasn't accomplished earlier."

Aloud she said, "Martin, would you please pass the potatoes?"

I was beside myself, but I knew that Eduardo was watching and listening to us all. A million questions swarmed through my mind.

"You're shouting mentally, Martin. Please get hold of yourself."

"But what about Eduardo?" I thought back. "Doesn't he hear us as well?"

"I think not. Something has happened to him since he has occupied the ODIN machine. It may be that his special abilities are a function of the body he inhabits. In his disembodied form, or inside the body which Henskey's coroner destroyed, he is, indeed, a paranormal giant. But inside the ODIN, he is merely a genius the like of which the world has never known. He has the world at his fingertips. But he cannot read thoughts. He is evidently no longer clairvoyant, either, or he would have foreseen my reaction to his mad plans of world domination. Or if he has foreseen my reaction, what little I am able to do about his ambitions is of no consequence."

"Then it doesn't matter, anyway," I thought. "For a single second, I thought there might be a way out of this nightmare."

"There may be, yet," she responded. "I may need your help tonight when the President comes to the computer display room. I will request that you be present. Watch and listen for my lead. I will key my move to the phrase: *Tell me of this new world, Eddie.*"

"Tell me of this new world, Eddie. I've got it."

An eerie disembodied laugh echoed inside my head. "Yes, I know. You forget nothing, my dear. I caught you thinking about that week we spent on Cape Cod." Color came to my cheeks. No one at the table noticed. They were rattling on about the President's impending visit. It was then it dawned on me that while she had been "talking" with me, Myra had also been keeping up her end of the conversation at the table!

I don't know what I contributed to the small talk after that. I'm sure I appeared a perfect fool. I couldn't help it. I kept thinking, "It can be learned! These powers can be acquired!" Somehow, the world didn't look nearly as grim as before lunch. But there is still tonight to come . . . What I'll do then, I don't know. I must trust Myra.

GEORGE CASE

Bless Henskey. When it came time for the introductions to the President, he didn't refer to me by name.

He only said, "And this is my top field agent, Mr. President." I don't think I could have taken it if I'd been introduced as "Stinky."

It was impressive to see the whole presidential entourage arrive. I guess I'm as square as the average citizen when it comes to the presidency. Even though I know a great deal more than the average voter when it comes to inside politics, when I saw the limousines come up the main drive, and the President's flag on the second car, I choked up.

I nearly went through the floor when I saw who was with him, though. The first time a president has been to Greenglade compound, and his honored guests are the Secretary of State, the Secretary of Defense, and Dimitri Gangov, the Russian Foreign Minister! I wouldn't have let Gangov within five miles of this place. But I guess, now, security is a thing of the past. It's a brand-new ball game with Rodriguez giving the orders and making up the rules as he goes along.

Henskey had detailed me to take charge of the Secret Service and Russian security escort. We'll sit around Area A until the proceedings down in the ODIN display room are over. For me, it's just as well. I wouldn't want to be there when Rodriguez starts giving orders to the man I've sworn to protect, and whose office I'm supposed to be upholding. I suppose the full responsibility falls on Henskey, as head of operations. I wonder how he'll handle it?

DARRYL HENSKEY

I wonder what the hell I'm going to do and say? There's no avoiding it now. It was different explaining the situation to the President that night at the White House. He took it well, if such an outrageous situation can be taken at all, let alone well. But actually, coming face-to-face with that *thing* in the basement . . . Then there's Gangov to be considered.

I knew the President was going to have a helluva time with the Russians. But to bring Gangov here! I guess it's the only way they'd believe what's happened. I still find it difficult, myself.

Sokolow is staying cool. She has a plan, all right. But she won't fill me in. All I know is that when we're assembled down in the ODIN console room, she's going to give me my cue. I have one line to speak. I think I know what she's going to try. I also thing she's dead wrong. She's putting all our lives on the line if she's miscalculated. If I were a praying man, I'd be on my knees right now.

MARTIN GROSSMAN

I've never loved Myra more. I've never been so proud of anyone as I was at that moment. I didn't know what she had in mind. It's just as well. Had I known, every indicator on Rodriguez's polygraph pickups would have gone over the line. She also trusted me enough to pick up her intent once she began to implement her plan. That was flattering in and of itself.

We were about to enter the ODIN display room after going through all the security hocus-pocus that would admit Gangov and the President. It seemed like a pointless process. After all, in twenty-four hours, such things would be ancient history. It was amusing to realize, though, that the President had no more clearance than the Russian foreign minister. But considering the fact that no president has ever come to this place, it's only natural that no provision had been made for him to be in the main console room.

I'd seen the President before. He addressed the faculty and student body last year when the university gave him that honorary degree. I was impressed with him then, and was again. It's easy to understand why some political writers call the presidency a popularity contest. I was unprepared for the sheer charm of the man, even under the terrible strain of his situation. He introduced Gangov to the rest of us as though he and the Russian were old school chums.

Evidently, the President had been well briefed on who we all were, He introduced me to Gangov as "professor-doctor" in the European style. And he was well aware of my credentials as well as my specialty. Gangov was a surprise. I'd only seen him on TV and was unprepared for the fact that he's well over six feet tall. He has great personal charm, and it's difficult to bear in mind that this man was responsible for the internment of so many Soviet Jews before he was named Foreign Minister. One can always think of a distant figure as an oppressor and a butcher. But when the butcher greets you and says, "Enchanted, Professor-doctor. Or would you prefer to be addressed as simply Professor?"

I was taken back and stammered, "Just doctor will do, Your Excellency."

Gangov smiled widely, showing a gold tooth I'd not noticed before. "In that event, 'Your Excellency' is not necessary. Such titles seem to please your politicians. You may call me 'Comrade Minister' or Dimitri, if you like."

"Thank you, Comrade Minister," I said.

He laughed deeply and put a hand on my shoulder. I couldn't help it, I shrank away from his touch. It didn't bother him in the slightest.

"Come now, Doctor," he said. "I don't have two heads. And I assure you I am a devoted family man. We are not the monsters your press would have you believe. And I am very interested in your field of research. We have been conducting research along these lines in the Soviet Union for years. Naturally, our program is well in advance of your own, as is our KALINSK VII computer superior to your ODIN in the next room. You see, we have no prejudices against pure research in my country. You should visit us someday and see for yourself what can be done when an entire government is behind your project."

I couldn't restrain myself when he said what he did about no prejudice in the Soviet Union. I said, "I doubt I'd be welcome, Comrade Minister. I am a Jew."

"And I am an atheist. Does that mean we cannot work together? I think you believe too much of what you read in your newspapers. True, we have had a certain amount of trouble with some malcontents and troublemakers who happen to be Jews. But there are many loyal Russians who are Jews and hold responsible positions in my country."

"How many in positions of real authority?" I asked.

Gangov smiled. "About as many as you have here in your more enlightened country. Oh, excuse me. I forgot about your recent Secretary of State."

We didn't get a chance to continue. The President came between us and without the slightest sign of discomfort, shifted the conversation back to introductions. Myra greeted Gangov with reserve. He responded in kind. The marine guard outside the room pressed the door release, and we entered the console display room where ODIN/Eduardo waited.

There had been a number of changes made since I first saw the room two weeks before. A set of wall-to-wall drapes now hid the display console from view. Arranged before the drapes in a semicircle were five padded metal frame chairs. I knew those chairs well. They were all tied into the main polygraph. Facing the semicircle of chairs, just in front of the drawn drapes, was a larger padded chair. Without a word, Myra went directly to this chair and sat down facing us.

"Please be seated, gentlemen," she said. "In a few minutes, you will be privileged to have an audience with Eduardo the First and Last, absolute ruler of the planet. You will address your questions to me. If you wish to speak directly to Eduardo, you must first ask my permission. If Eduardo speaks to you directly and requires a response, you will address him as Lord God."

"Absurd!" snorted Gangov from where he sat.

"IS IT, COMRADE GANGOV?"

Rodriguez had modified the ODIN speaker system somehow. The voice that came through the speakers was now less mechanical. But it was set to a diapason bass register with a heavy degree of reverb built in. As a piece of showmanship, designed to impress, it was superb. It sounded, indeed, like the voice of some wrathful deity.

It went on, "DO YOU STILL THINK IT ABSURD, COMRADE?"

I looked over at Gangov. He was completely immobile, his hands gripping the arms of his metal chair. Sweat beaded his brow.

"A SIMPLE DEVICE, COMRADE. A LIGHT ELECTRICAL CURRENT. IT WILL IMMOBILIZE AT THIS LEVEL. AT HIGHER LEVELS, IT CAN CAUSE EXQUISITE PAIN. AND IF I CHOOSE, IT CAN KILL. A SIMPLE PLEASURE/PAIN DEVICE. IF YOU DISOBEY, YOU ARE PUNISHED, AS NOW. IF YOU PLEASE ME . . ."

I couldn't take my eyes off Gangov. Now, his face wore an expression of delight, even euphoria.

"YOU SEE, COMRADE? ISN'T IT MUCH BETTER TO PLEASE ME THAN TO RISK MY WRATH? I'M SURE YOU CAN APPRECIATE HOW THIS WORKS. AFTER ALL, IT DERIVES FROM PAVLOV. NOW YOU JUST BE A GOOD LITTLE COMRADE, AND WE'LL HAVE NO MORE DIFFICULTIES. UNDERSTAND?"

"Yes, Lord God Eduardo."

"MUCH BETTER. AH, I SEE WE ARE ALL HERE. I ASSUME THAT GANGOV IS PRESENT BECAUSE HE WOULDN'T BELIEVE I EXIST. NO MATTER. BY TOMORROW, WHAT ANY MORTAL THINKS WILL NO LONGER MATTER. MYRA, WILL YOU DRAW THE DRAPES?"

Myra got up and slid the draperies that concealed the main console to one side. The display board was no longer fully visible. Before it was a large video-beam. The room darkened and the screen lit up. For the first time, I saw the face of Eduardo the First. It was ingenious what he had done.

The image on the screen was a three-dimensional representation of an idealized young man's face. I know little of electronics, but I have seen such things before. It wasn't a moving picture, but a constantly changing line drawing. It gave the illusion of looking at whomever it was speaking to. I knew full well that Rodriguez was "seeing us" through a series of video monitors all around the room. But as an effect, it was excellent. It gave the impression of a figure twice as big as life, and impossibly regal.

Myra had taken her seat again and was regarding us all with an air of utmost serenity. "Gentlemen, the audience will now begin. We will commence with any questions the President has."

The President got to his feet. "Dr. Sokolow. I am aware of all demands made by Eduardo the First. I am also cognizant of his abilities to carry out the threats he has made. I have, however, been unable to convince the Foreign Minister of the seriousness of the situation. He believes this all to be an elaborate plan for U.S. world domination. How may he be convinced otherwise?"

"I HAVE NO RESPONSIBILITY TO THE SOVIET UNION TO CONVINCE THEM OF MY EXISTENCE. THE MINISTER MAY INFER FROM THE DESTRUCTION OF A FEW MAJOR RUSSIAN CITIES THAT I AM SINCERE. THE FACT THAT REPRISALS WILL BE MADE BY THE SOVIET UNION DOES NOT CONCERN ME. I AM SAFE HERE FROM ANY ATTACK. THE ENTIRE PLANET CAN BE DESTROYED. I STILL SHALL SURVIVE. HOWEVER, IF IT WOULD FACILITATE MATTERS, I COULD JUST AS EASILY DESTROY A FEW MAJOR

AMERICAN CITIES AS WELL. IT'S OF SECONDARY IM-
PORTANCE TO ME."

I heard a sharp intake of breath from the Secretary of Defense, who was seated beside me.

Then Gangov addressed Myra. "Am I to understand that Eduardo the First will destroy the planet
for a whim?"

"That is correct," Myra answered.

"How do I know that this is not a . . . bluff? Is that
the word?"

"YOU DO NOT KNOW IF IT IS A BLUFF. I DON'T
CARE ONE WAY OR ANOTHER. IT IS ONLY BECAUSE I
AM NOT A TOTALLY UNFEELING GOD THAT I HAVE
AFFORDED YOU THIS OPPORTUNITY TO SURVIVE. I
CAN BE MERCIFUL."

Gangov was not to be denied his logic. He pressed
on, still addressing Myra. "If I can be given sufficient
assurance that this is not a ruse on the part of the
United States government, I can report the demands
to my government for their consideration. I can do
no more."

"I think once you hear the nature of the demands,"
Myra said, "any doubts you have will be resolved.
What is required of all governments of the world
is clearly not in keeping with U.S. policy."

"YOU WASTE TIME, MYRA. EITHER COMRADE GAN-
GOV CAPITULATES OR HIS COUNTRY WILL BE DE-
STROYED. HE HAS HIS CHOICE: MY WORLD TO BE, OR
THE COMPLETE DESTRUCTION OF HIS WORLD AS IT IS."

I almost missed my lead. Myra brought off the key
phrase so naturally in conversation that it nearly
went by me. She said quietly, "I think all his doubts
could be cleared up if you will tell us of this new
world, Eduardo."

"VERY WELL. AS A FAVOR TO YOU, MY CONSORT,

133

MYRA. I HAVE NO NEED TO EXPLAIN OTHERWISE. TO BEGIN WITH, ALL POLITICAL BOUNDARIES WILL BE ABOLISHED AND THERE WILL BE FREE TRAVEL BETWEEN NATIONS. ALL STANDING ARMIES ARE TO BE DISBANDED. ALL MONIES ALLOCATED FOR WEAPONS ARE TO BE DIVERTED INTO MEDICAL RESEARCH UNDER MY DIRECTION. THE PRIMARY PROJECTS WILL BE THE COMPLETE ERADICATION OF DISEASE AND HUNGER IN THE WORLD.

ALL CURRENT HEADS OF GOVERNMENT, AFTER A PERIOD OF ADJUSTMENT TO MY REIGN, WILL RESIGN. MY FORMULA FOR WORLD GOVERNMENT WILL BE PROMULGATED THROUGH THEM. AFTER THAT TIME, THEY WILL NO LONGER BE NECESSARY. SECRET POLICE, SUCH AS THE ORGANIZATION IN WHOSE HEADQUARTERS WE MET, WILL ALSO BE DISBANDED. AFTER A SHORT TIME, ALL MONEY SYSTEMS WILL BE DISCARDED AND A UNIVERSAL CREDIT SCHEME WILL BE SUBSTITUTED. THERE WILL BE ONE GOVERNMENT: MINE. THROUGH THIS MACHINE WHICH I INHABIT, I AM ABLE TO HEAR THE GRIEVANCES OF ALL AND METE OUT JUSTICE SIMULTANEOUSLY ALL OVER THE WORLD. ANY OF MY SUBJECTS WILL HAVE ACCESS TO THEIR GOVERNMENT, THEIR GOD, THEIR BENEFACTOR, THEIR TASKMASTER, AND ENFORCER. FOR I SHALL BE ALL THESE THINGS.

RESISTANCE TO MY RULE WILL BE IMPOSSIBLE FOR THE SIMPLEST OF REASONS. TO DISOBEY WILL MEAN DEATH AND DESTRUCTION FOR ALL. YOU WILL SEE, EACH OF YOU, THAT ALL OBEY. I DON'T HAVE NEED FOR POLICE. ANY DISOBEDIENCE TO MY COMMANDS WILL RESULT IN THE DEVASTATION OF THE AREA FROM WHICH THE DISOBEDIENCE COMES. PERHAPS A FEW OBJECT LESSONS WILL BE NECESSARY AT FIRST, BUT IN THE LONG RUN, ALL WILL COMPLY.

AND WE WILL FEED THIS WORLD IN THE WISEST OF

134

WAYS. WE SHALL CONTROL THE BIRTHRATE. PERMIS-
SION TO REPRODUCE WILL BE GRANTED TO THOSE WHO
ARE GENETICALLY SOUND AND ARE WILLING TO MAKE
A CONTRIBUTION TO THE BETTERMENT OF MY WORLD.

THIS PART WILL PLEASE COMRADE GANGOV. THERE
WILL BE NO MORE PERSONAL PROPERTY. ALL THAT
EXISTS IS MINE, AND MY SUBJECTS WILL RECEIVE
RANK AND PRIVILEGE IN DIRECT PROPORTON TO THEIR
LOYALTY AND CONTRIBUTION TO MY WORLD. BUT THEY
CAN NEVER BECOME AN ELITE GROUP. BECAUSE I AM
ABLE TO ADMINISTER ALL ASPECTS OF GOVERNMENT
PERFECTLY AND SIMULTANEOUSLY, THERE WILL BE NO
NEED FOR A JUDICIARY OR ANY LEGISLATIVE BODY.
AND NO ONE WILL INHERIT PROPERTY OR RANK. EACH
INDIVIDUAL WILL DETERMINE HIS OWN FUTURE AND
WILL BE REWARDED FOR HIS EFFORTS REGARDLESS OF
HIS ORIGINS, LANGUAGE OR RACE. THIS IS HOW IT
WILL BE. IT WILL BE SO, FOR I WISH IT TO BE SO. THERE
IS SO MUCH MORE, BUT I HAVE NO NEED NOR DESIRE
TO EXPLAIN THESE OTHER THINGS TO YOU. I HAVE
SPOKEN."

I sat there, aghast. Any doubt I had about
Eduardo's sanity was now resolved. But to tell the
truth, there was a great deal to his grand plan that
didn't displease me.

Myra spoke again. "But perhaps, Eddie, inhabiting
the machine as you do may make you less sensitive
to the needs of us poor humans. We are bound to the
frailties of our bodies. You are immortal in your
body of steel, concrete, and circuitry. Can this not
make you more mechanical in your judgments, less
human?" She paused. "I ask this not for myself. I
merely wish the others to understand so that you
may start your reign with a minimum of bloodshed."

"WELL SPOKEN, MYRA. AS YOU KNOW, I HAVE

MADE YOU MY CONSORT SO THAT I MAY NOT LOSE TOUCH WITH THE MASS OF HUMANITY. YOU ARE THE MOST COMPASSIONATE HUMAN I HAVE KNOWN. AS TO BECOMING LESS THAN HUMAN, HOW CAN THAT BE, WHEN I AM ALREADY SO MUCH MORE THAN HUMAN?"

"But it is this computer body of yours that makes you more than human. Does it not make demands on you that drive you away from the human condition? Can you sympathize with a human who is ill when you never know illness? More than that, can you share grief when you will never know loss? Is there not a danger that you will in time become more and more the machine you inhabit? How much of you is now machine? How much of your responses are electronic and mechanical? We have long argued that mentality is a function of the body. And your body is mechanical."

"AS IS YOURS, DEAR MYRA. DO YOU CONSCIOUSLY CONTROL YOUR BREATHING OR HEARTBEAT, THE OPENING AND CLOSING OF YOUR PORES, THE FLOW OF YOUR HORMONES? OR DO YOU ONLY THINK OF YOUR BODY WHEN IT DOES NOT FUNCTION PROPERLY? THE PART OF ME THAT IS ODIN FUNCTIONS SUPERBLY, DOING ALL THAT IT WAS MEANT TO DO. IN THE SAME WAY THAT YOUR BODY FUNCTIONS IN THOUSANDS OF WAYS TO HOUSE YOUR MENTALITY WITHOUT YOUR BEING AWARE OF IT, SO DOES MINE. I ENJOY THE EQUIVALENT OF AN AUTONOMIC NERVOUS SYSTEM. EXCEPT I FEEL NO PAIN. I RECEIVE A SIGNAL THAT A CERTAIN AREA OF MY BODY NEEDS REPAIR. WITHOUT ANY CONSCIOUS EFFORT ON MY PART, DRONE SERVICE MACHINES REPAIR IT. MY INTERNAL MAINTENANCE SYSTEM IS FAR SUPERIOR TO YOURS."

I was rapt. But I heard Myra's voice inside my head say, "Ask him how he took control of ODIN and got past all security. It would be a logical question for the Russian to ask."

I addressed the question to Myra. "Dr. Sokolow. Perhaps Comrade Gangov would understand more fully if he knew how Eduardo the First was able to fool the entire I.G.O. and take over such a machine. I feel if he knew what we do about Eduardo the First, all his doubts about a U.S. plot would be resolved."

"I SEE FROM YOUR BODY READINGS THAT YOU ARE NERVOUS, DR. GROSSMAN. THERE IS NO NEED. I WON'T TURN OUT THE LIGHTS. BUT YOUR POINT IS WELL TAKEN. I TOOK CONTROL OF ODIN BY GAINING ACCESS TO THIS ROOM IN THE BODY OF A YOUNG MAN NAMED ORTIZ. I RODE IN HERE INSIDE HIS BODY AS YOU WOULD RIDE IN AN AUTOMOBILE. ORTIZ WAS AUTHORIZED TO BE HERE. NO ONE QUESTIONED ME AS ORTIZ. ONCE INSIDE, I QUIT ORTIZ'S BODY AND ENTERED ODIN. ODIN HAD NO PROGRAMMED DEFENSE AGAINST MY DOING SO. HOW COULD IT? SUCH A THING HAD NEVER BEEN THOUGHT OF.

Before I realized what was happening, Henskey jumped to his feet. He pointed a finger at the image on the screen and said, "Ortiz was authorized personnel. Eduardo Rodriguez was never authorized to be in here, or to operate ODIN. You are unauthorized personnel! ODIN: Destruct!" Then all hell broke loose.

A siren began to sound, and an overhead red light started flashing. The door to the room burst open, and the marine guard charged in, service automatic drawn. We all stood in our places as though frozen.

Henskey was the first to speak. "You've had it, Rodriguez," shouted. "You can't use your missiles, now. You can't use anything. In another fifty seconds

137

there won't be anything left of you. You'll just sit there in your mechanical coffin and wait for the end. But before it comes, this is from me to Lord God Eduardo the First and Last!" And with that, Henskey faced the screen and blew it the fattest razzberry I've heard since I left the Bronx!

There was dead silence in the room for a second, then Rodriguez spoke once more over the sound system. His last words were, "MYRA, DEAR MYRA, YOU, TOO."

Then the lights on the screen and the console behind it grew very bright. And went out.

INTERIM REPORT: EYES ONLY

To: The President of the United States

From: D. F. Henskey, District Supervisor, I.G.O. HQ, Greenglade, MD.

Re: NIETZSCHE

Dear Mr. President:

At your order, the ODIN complex is being dismantled. During the time necessary to restore adequate national defense measures, we are keeping all stations on a red alert status. We estimate the conversion back to conventional defense systems will take eighteen months to two years. Our experts say that we can't salvage anything from the ODIN but some lesser components. They also say we could have kept the whole country on red alert for fifteen years for the cost of building a new computer of the ODIN class.

As to my opinion on Gangov keeping his mouth shut, I trust him as far as I can throw the Kremlin. Mr. President, we simply have to face up to the fact that one of the highest ranking Russians in the world has seen all our secrets, and is under no obligation whatever to keep quiet about it to his superiors, or the world press for that matter.

I suppose we could deny that ODIN ever existed. After all, the only evidence to prove it did is three-quarters of an acre of very expensive junk down below the HQ building.

It was good of you to inquire as to the status of agent Ortiz. A day after the ODIN self-destructed, he began to come out of it. Drs. Grossman and Sokolow say he'll be as good as new soon.

Sokolow and Grossman present something of a problem to us just now. They have been privy to as much as the Russian. There can be no doubt as to Grossman's loyalty; he was cleared and has acted as a consultant for us in the past. Sokolow is something else. She wants to return to her practice in New York. We have no more legal means for keeping her here than we did Guzman, who was released last week. I offered her a post with the Agency, so we could keep tabs on her, but she turned it down. She has promised me personally that she has no interest in making any of the events of the past weeks public. Short of having her taken out, I can't do more than I have. Please advise on this aspect.

I am recommending that George Case be advanced to Grade 9 and given the post of Western District Supervisor. Our man there is due for retirement next year, anyway.

As it now stands, the only people who know that the whole crazy thing happened are yourself, the two Secretaries, Case, Ortiz, Sokolow, Grossman, and myself. And the Russian, of course.

I would also like to thank you for declining to accept my resignation. You're right. There was no way of foreseeing such a thing taking place, and the Agency couldn't have been blamed for not having a defense against it. I shall try in the future to be worthy of your trust in me and I.G.O.

Sincerely,
D.F. Henskey

MARTIN GROSSMAN

I can't believe it's over. Just like that. As Myra explained it to me, she took a calculated risk. She gambled that the bulk of the ODIN computer was functioning as it always had. The reason that the enmergency cutoff hadn't functioned before was that there was no call for it. So far as the ODIN was concerned, only authorized personnel had been in the console room. Though Eduardo was an outsider, he entered in the guise of Ortiz, who was authorized. The computer was not programmed to handle such a situation since there was no precedent. So when it was explained to the computer that an unauthorized person was giving it orders, the cutout functioned, and ODIN destroyed itself. Myra says her only regret is that Eddie was destroyed in the process.

I can't in all truth shed too many tears over the passing of Eduardo the First. True, there were a few plans that he had for the future of the world that seemed attractive. But if one looks at the histories of the most vicious totalitarians the world has known, they have begun with promises like Eduardo's.

What excites me most is Myra acquiring telepathic abilities! If she can, perhaps so can others. I'm certainly going to try. Unfortunately, she doesn't seem to know how Rodriguez did it. All she can say is that it felt as though he reached inside her and turned on a switch. That's not much to work with, but more than I had a month ago.

Myra has agreed to let me join her in New York. She has responsibilities to her patients. I, on the other hand, have only my research on paranormal phenomena at the university. I can learn more in a week observing Myra's talents than I have since I began my work three years ago. Myers, my assistant, can take my classes. I think he's always wanted the job, anyway.

I realize that I can't be more than an associate to Myra. How can one offer more to a person who has been confidante to a mind like Rodriguez's? But there's always the chance that the telepathic ability can be passed on to others! I must make this effort. If I succeed, then perhaps Myra and I can share more than our work. I hope so. I've never cared more for anyone in my life.

And it just may be that our work will be the beginning of that future history of which Myra spoke—the telepathic breakthrough that paved the way to understanding among all the children of this planet. Against the hope that it will be, I'm ready to spend the rest of my life and energies working toward the end. With Myra's help, it promises to be most rewarding in any number of ways.

The New York Times

Gangov Resigns Post As Soviet Foreign Minister

MOSCOW, October 15—Soviet news agency Tass reported today that Dimitri Gangov, for five years Foreign Minister, has resigned his post for reasons of "ill health."

Mr. Gangov, whose career spanned over twenty-five years and three regimes, was lauded by Tass as "a great statesman and true revolutionary." He is to be awarded the decoration of Hero of The People, First Order, in a formal ceremony later this month.

DARRYL HENSKEY

It didn't seem smart to tell the President that Sokolow can read minds. I'd have also had to tell him that she knows exactly how the I.G.O. is set up. After all, Sokolow is an apolitical person. She's only using the talent to help cure her patients. Understand that she and Grossman are quite the pair these days. Maybe she's cured that claustrophobia of his.

Aida Ruiz has turned up. She ran scared after the

Oritz interview and had been living in the basement of a storefront church in Spanish Harlem for four weeks. Someone might believe her if she told the story. But face it, whoever she tells can't matter to us or the Agency.

But now this. I just got a report from one of our agents behind the Curtain that Gangov has gone insane. They're keeping him under wraps at a home near the Black Sea. Our operative says he went nutty the same day he got back to Moscow. So far as we know, he didn't have a chance to spill it about the ODIN/NIETZSCHE fiasco.

But my real worry is the nature of his madness. Our agent says that he's like a vegetable. Physically, he's healthy as a man his age can be. But upstairs, nobody home. I keep thinking about the sixty-second countdown before the ODIN blew. Did Rodriguez have time to get out? I wish I knew!

GLOSSARY

barrio (m.) District, neighborhood; slang, Spanish ghetto

bolita (f.) Lottery; Spanish numbers racket

chulo (m.) Pimp

comprender (v.) To understand, grasp

gringa (f.) English-speaking woman

gringo (m.) English-speaking man

jefe (m.) Chief

Latino (m.) Latin person

los tigres (m. pl.) The tigers (*tigre* (m.) Tiger)

¿Que tal? How are you?

salsa (f.) Puerto Rican rock music; Puerto Rican dancing style

un hombre de honor A man of honor

ABOUT THE AUTHOR

T. ERNESTO BETHANCOURT is also known as singer-guitarist Tom Paisley, who began his career in coffee-houses in Greenwich Village in the sixties, performing with then unknowns Bob Dylan, Bill Cosby, and Peter, Paul, and Mary. He has served as a contributing editor to *High Fidelity Magazine*, and is the author of two highly acclaimed young adult novels, *New York City Too Far from Tampa Blues* and *The Dog Days of Arthur Cane*. He lives in Brooklyn, New York, with his wife and two daughters.

DAHL, ZINDEL, BLUME AND BRANCATO

Select the best names, the best stories in the world of teenage and young readers books!

- ☐ 15030 CHARLIE AND THE CHOCOLATE FACTORY $1.95
  Roald Dahl
- ☐ 15031 CHARLIE AND THE GREAT GLASS $1.95
  ELEVATOR   Roald Dahl
- ☐ 15035 DANNY THE CHAMPION OF THE WORLD $1.95
  Roald Dahl
- ☐ 15032 JAMES AND THE GIANT PEACH   Roald Dahl $1.95
- ☐ 12154 THE WONDERFUL STORY OF HENRY $1.95
  SUGAR AND SIX MORE   Roald Dahl
- ☐ 12579 THE PIGMAN   Paul Zindel $1.95
- ☐ 12774 I NEVER LOVED YOUR MIND   Paul Zindel $1.95
- ☐ 12501 PARDON ME, YOU'RE STEPPING ON MY $1.95
  EYEBALL!   Paul Zindel
- ☐ 12741 MY DARLING, MY HAMBURGER $1.95
  Paul Zindel
- ☐ 11829 CONFESSIONS OF A TEENAGE BABOON $1.95
  Paul Zindel
- ☐ 13628 IT'S NOT THE END OF THE WORLD $1.95
  Judy Blume
- ☐ 13693 WINNING   Robin Brancato $1.95
- ☐ 12171 SOMETHING LEFT TO LOSE $1.75
  Robin Brancato
- ☐ 12953 BLINDED BY THE LIGHT   Robin Brancato $1.95

Buy them at your local bookstore or use this handy coupon for ordering:

TEENAGERS FACE LIFE AND LOVE

Choose books filled with fun and adventure, discovery and disenchantment, failure and conquest, triumph and tragedy life and love.

☐	13359	**THE LATE GREAT ME** Sandra Scoppettone	$1.95
☐	13691	**HOME BEFORE DARK** Sue Ellen Bridgers	$1.75
☐	11961	**THE GOLDEN SHORES OF HEAVEN** Katie Letcher Lyle	$1.50
☐	12501	**PARDON ME, YOU'RE STEPPING ON MY EYEBALL!** Paul Zindel	$1.95
☐	11091	**A HOUSE FOR JONNIE O.** Blossom Elfman	$1.95
☐	12025	**ONE FAT SUMMER** Robert Lipsyte	$1.75
☐	13184	**I KNOW WHY THE CAGED BIRD SINGS** Maya Angelou	$2.25
☐	13013	**ROLL OF THUNDER, HEAR MY CRY** Mildred Taylor	$1.95
☐	12741	**MY DARLING, MY HAMBURGER** Paul Zindel	$1.95
☐	12420	**THE BELL JAR** Sylvia Plath	$2.50
☐	12338	**WHERE THE RED FERN GROWS** Wilson Rawls	$1.75
☐	11829	**CONFESSIONS OF A TEENAGE BABOON** Paul Zindel	$1.95
☐	11632	**MARY WHITE** Caryl Ledner	$1.95
☐	13352	**SOMETHING FOR JOEY** Richard E. Peck	$1.95
☐	13440	**SUMMER OF MY GERMAN SOLDIER** Bette Greene	$1.95
☐	13693	**WINNING** Robin Brancato	$1.95
☐	13628	**IT'S NOT THE END OF THE WORLD** Judy Blume	$1.95

Buy them at your local bookstore or use this handy coupon for ordering:

Bantam Books, Inc., Dept. EDN, 414 East Golf Road, Des Plaines, Ill. 60016

Please send me the books I have checked above. I am enclosing $_____ (please add 75¢ to cover postage and handling). Send check or money order —no cash or C.O.D.'s please.

Mr/Mrs/Miss _____

Address _____

City _____ State/Zip _____

EDN—12/79

Please allow four weeks for delivery. This offer expires 6/80.

WHEN YOU THINK ZINDEL, THINK BANTAM!

If you like novels whose characters are teenagers caught in the tangle of life and love—PAUL ZINDEL is right on your wavelength. All of Zindel's Young Adult novels are now available exclusively from Bantam.

☐	12501	PARDON ME, YOU'RE STEPPING ON MY EYEBALL!	$1.95
☐	12741	MY DARLING, MY HAMBURGER	$1.95
☐	11829	CONFESSIONS OF A TEENAGE BABOON	$1.95
☐	12579	THE PIGMAN	$1.95
☐	12774	I NEVER LOVED YOUR MIND	$1.95
☐	12548	THE EFFECT OF GAMMA RAYS ON MAN-IN-THE-MOON MARIGOLDS	$1.95

MS READ-a-thon—
a simple way
to start youngsters reading.

Boys and girls between 6 and 14 can join the MS READ-a-thon and help find a cure for Multiple Sclerosis by reading books. And they get two rewards — the enjoyment of reading, and the great feeling that comes from helping others.

Parents and educators: For complete information call your local MS chapter, or call toll-free (800) 243-6000. Or mail the coupon below.

Kids can help, too!